RIVER OF GHOSTS

A
HAUNTED FLORIDA
NOVEL

GABY TRIANA

RIVER OF GHOSTS

ONE

1719

Through his warped spyglass, Captain Bellamy gazed at the silhouette against the setting sun and snorted with disgust. "*Córdoba*! She sails at us!"

"Take action, sir?" Newell asked.

As the sun sank toward tangerine waters, Bellamy gritted his teeth. He couldn't let the *Córdoba* get away a second time. "Prepare to intercept!"

"Aye, aye, Captain."

Bellamy lowered his spyglass to watch his crew, as the deck of the *Vanquish* bustled in preparation for battle.

"Seven bells!" The watch rang out 2-2-2-1.

"Sounding?" Newell called.

One frazzled seaman gathered rope and lifted the plummet. "By the mark of three."

"Shallows, sir," Newell said to Bellamy. "We have the keel, but the *Córdoba* is overloaded. Gold, most likely."

Bellamy peered through his spyglass again, gaze transfixed on the distant Spanish galleon. He pointed northward at the treacherous sandbars of the Floridian islands. "Then it is our duty to relieve them of their burden. We'll ground her there. Come about smartly."

"Aye, aye, Captain. Look sharp." Newell snapped his fingers at the coxswain whose thick arms turned the

1

ship's wheel larboard, cutting *Vanquish*'s hull through the heaves of the shallow straits.

Bellamy dug his fingers into the bridge's rail and waited. Its splintered surface told of his ship's last engagement with *Córdoba* when she'd escaped by the skin of her teeth. "She gave us the slip last. To be certain, she'll not get away again."

He turned back and addressed his startled crew.

"Hear me! No quarter. Tonight, you men will earn your share of gold!"

Cheers erupted, as the lower deck burst into another frenzy of preparation, transferring powder from the dry magazines below and stacking cannonballs.

"Round-shot?" Newell asked the captain.

Bellamy sneered. "Bolas, my friend. Tear her apart enough to cease sail, not to spoil her treasures."

"Aye, Captain." Newell grinned in approval. "Chain-shot, it is!"

"One thousand yards!" the watch called.

Bellamy smacked the rails. "Boom us about. We'll careen her aground."

Córdoba's great sails overflowed with volumes of wind, but she could not alter her course in enough time to escape the *Vanquish*. Bellamy gazed patiently at the merchant vessel filled with treasure that would soon be his.

"Come to me, bilge rats. Come to this watery grave of eternal damnation." He laughed under his breath.

"Five-hundred!" the watch announced.

The captain's nerves sizzled like a lit fuse, as his point of view scanned back and forth along the enemy ship's rails.

Suddenly, he caught sight of an unmistakable shape—a young woman standing intrepidly at *Córdoba*'s bow in flowing green garb. A female aboard a merchant ship? *Córdoba*'s captain truly *did* wish to die an unlucky death. He was nearly asking for it.

The beautiful creature sent a signal. With chin up high and orange tendrils flailing around her face, she lifted two fingers in a rude gesture. Bellamy was taken aback. Damnation, once he eliminated the enemy crew, he would not—*could* not—entertain this woman aboard his ship as prisoner. Such would be bad luck for everyone.

"Very well, sassy wench, you'll be last to die," Bellamy mumbled.

"Two-hundred!"

"FIRE!" Bellamy's command ripped through the decks.

Reflexively, the gunners set their igniters to the cannon fuse, and the blasts rumbled across the decks. *Vanquish*'s eighteen-pound shot shattered *Córdoba*'s weakened sides. The ship wallowed like a sow in mud and lurched at every iron punch. Chain-shots burst from cannon muzzles twirling skyward.

Direct hit.

Each of *Córdoba*'s three masts buckled and snapped, her tattered sails billowing like death sheets over the ship's broken body.

More chain shots blasted from *Vanquish*'s formidable cannons. The engagement lasted but two minutes, a stark contrast to the hour of last encounter. Marksmen, high in the ship's rigging, eliminated most officers, even piercing the cannon ports, felling gunners and loaders. Sulfuric clouds transmuted into an ominous fog, plunging the Spanish ship into a suffocating curtain-fall.

Bellamy held a hand in the air to cease fire, for he was not a brutal man.

He waited to assess the damaged ship. He did not wish the enemy vessel sinking below the water, or all would be lost. Silence settled over the straits. The ringing in his assaulted ears lingered.

Suddenly, the fiery glow of the setting sun gave way to blazing tentacles of *Córdoba*'s powder magazines. The enemy crew abandoned their doomed ship, leaping into the water, flailing, screaming curses, begging for life, many impaling themselves on splintered debris in misguided efforts to avoid capture.

Bellamy smiled. "Scramble aboard and save what you can. Run out the plank!" he ordered, turning to the helm. "Where's my boatswain? Where the hellfire is Knox? Do not let that ship go down!"

Knox grimaced, a disheveled man in a blue and red jacket with stolen Commodore rank markings. He scrambled up the aft steps holding a shimmering sabre. "Here, Captain. Me and Smith...we was down below. We, eh, knew you'd want this sharp and handsome."

The captain took the sabre and spun it about in quick swings, testing its aptitude. Abruptly, a massive impact shook the *Vanquish*, sending several men tumbling to the deck as the captain hung onto the railing. "What the devil is it now?"

A black cloud rose starboard side. Embers fluttered like fireflies in a field of soot, the glow of the blaze spreading across the water's surface. From the charred remains of the *Córdoba*, crew members of the *Vanquish* worked diligently to save the merchant ship's cargo.

From his own lower deck, a seaman called up to Bellamy. "Sir! *Córdoba*'s captain set her magazines—and his self—ablaze. These are all who survived."

Shouts of anguish and rage filled the pungent air, as Bellamy glanced down to see fifteen Spanish crewmen, and that one blasted woman, staggering across his deck, chains and shackles weighing down their hands and feet.

"And the gold?" Bellamy asked.

"Has all sunken, Captain. But these are shallow waters, and—"

"I know that, fool!" Bellamy shouted.

Blasted cannons. He hadn't intended to rip them apart. Whose fault had it been, though, for giving *Vanquish* aggressive chase on their previous meeting? He would have to return at sunrise to salvage the sunken treasure. And here, he'd hoped to sail back to Port Royal tonight, victory under his plumed hat.

Bellamy pointed his sabre at the unlucky lot. "Line them up on the larboard rails, then put a league between us and that scow." He frowned at the crew, especially at the woman whose wet, ginger locks reflected the fire emanating off the waves. "You will pay for this trouble."

Blasted woman.

His quarter master and boatswain scrambled from the helm, lining the weary prisoners against the rails. All manners of odor spoiled the fresh ocean scent, from stale sweat of the damned crew, both his and his captives, to the sulfur of cannons.

Bellamy strolled the length of prisoners from his high position of the upper deck. "You gave us trouble once before," he told them. "And again tonight. Now look at the result. I assume it wasn't worth it?"

His heavy boots descended the bridge ladder, as his gaze followed the smoldering carcass of the Spanish galleon sinking into the straits. A bright flash washed over the *Vanquish*, and Bellamy flinched in preparation for the *Córdoba*'s final concussion.

Yes, they would return to retrieve the gold in the morning, though it would have been infinitely simpler to carry it ship-to-ship, rather than sacrifice his valuable crew to the bottom of the sea like shark food.

Bellamy paced before the sixteen fearful prisoners, but only one dared to stare into his gaze—the same wench who'd given him rude gesture aboard her master's ship. Gauging from her fine threads and features, he gathered she'd been the captain's wife. He paused, slipping the point of his sabre underneath her chin.

"*¿Quién eres, diablo?*" the woman asked.

"Pardon, madame, but I seem to have left my Spanish dictionary in my cabin." Bellamy laughed, examining her facial features. Proud nose, bright green eyes, lovely lips. A fine creature indeed. Shame he would have to dispose of her.

"Who are you to declare war upon *Córdoba de España?*" Her English was quite good to his surprise, and her accent sent a thrill through his loins.

Bellamy reached into his coat and held up an envelope sealed with red wax and royal impression. "By the word and seal of His Majesty King George the First, I hold this letter of marque."

He approached the woman and waved the envelope at her face.

"So *I* ask—who are *you*, woman, to query?" He put the letter back in his coat then lifted his sabre, its point shifting aside the hair obscuring her delicate face.

"*Mi nombre es* María Pilar Carmona, wife of Capitán Agustín Lara of *Córdoba*." She spoke in heaving breaths, her voice laced with heartbreak, eyes rimmed with tears. "Why would you lay waste our ship, my husband's life…why, *capitán*?"

"Well, if it pleases you…" Bellamy suppressed a smile. "I'll have his remains raised alongside the gold tomorrow morning."

The woman's eyebrows drew together. "Gold? *Córdoba* carries no gold or treasures of worth. Any precious cargo sank in the fog of México during the storm we encountered. We were simply making our way back home." She began cracking a laugh then held it back, as if realizing the mistake too late.

Bellamy's chest filled with ire at her mockery. He was a good captain who tried to be kind. After all, he'd saved most of the enemy crew, including the bad luck charm herself, had he not? And here she was, making a fool of him?

Without another thought, he brought down his sabre and sliced off the wench's ear, sending the fleshy appendage spattering onto his pristine deck. A crewman picked it up and tossed it overboard. The woman cried out in agony, pressing a pretty hand to the side of her head, as blood splashed across the faces of the men chained beside her.

Mockery! He would have known of this storm, as most wended their way west from the eastern reaches of the ocean. She spoke of a storm borne from curse.

Bellamy was many things—a fine captain, a kind man, and a brother when needed—but one thing he was not was tolerant of witchcraft.

"Do not play with me, sorceress. Your life is forfeit, worth less to me than a full spittoon." Bellamy jabbed his sabre between her breasts. He did not trust women, especially ones who cackled at his misfortune. To the prisoner beside her, he asked, "This be true? The gold was lost at sea?"

He moved his sabre to the man's neck.

The poor seaman shuddered as if caught in winter's blizzard. "*Sí, capitán.* It is gone. The storm, it bore down on us, and—" Bellamy plunged through his flesh, lacerating his neck, as dark blood sprayed across the witch's voluptuous figure.

She covered her face. "*¿Diós mío, pero por qué?*" she screamed.

Bellamy could not contain his patience any longer. First, *Córdoba* had given him heavy chase, then they'd returned to taunt him with no pleasures for the taking. Now, her crew mocked him.

"I condemn you all to die this night." He shook with rage and slapped the woman's cheek with his blade. "And you, sorceress, shall watch them, one by one, and be the last to die."

Her tears carved rivers through her blood-stained face, as emerald eyes burned with scorn. "In this case, you shall suffer before dawn," she said in a hateful tone. Had this woman no remorse for her actions? "As above, so below, and within…you shall suffer and never see the sun again."

"Quiet!" he shouted, enraged for losing his patience. But her curse echoed in his mind, and for a moment, Bellamy wondered if truth might exist in her words. He wasn't normally a superstitious man, but when it came to women…

He thought of tipping her chin up with his fingers but reconsidered the touch. "Strong words coming from reptile food. What be the time?" he called out.

"By the bell, a half-and-twenty." A crewman struck the bell 2-2-1.

"Take us to the corals of the bay," Bellamy ordered Newell.

"Aye, Captain."

The great ship cut starboard, due north, toward the mainland.

He turned back to the Spanish woman—the Red Witch, he would always remember her. "You have one bell to make peace with God before eternal slumber welcomes you."

"I know no God." She glared at him, as he turned back to his bridge to watch the spectacle unfold. *No God? A witch indeed.*

The half moon loomed in the twilit sky casting a bloody pall over the seas, as the *Vanquish* sailed into the shallows. Crows and gulls swooped in great arcs above the masts, vultures of the sea waiting to gorge, and Bellamy was in a generous mood to feed them.

Soon another bell rang out, and the captain readied to discharge the prisoner's sentence. He pointed to the seaman standing beside the slain prisoner. "You. You shall be first to walk. Go, then."

The prisoner spoke through his tears. "*Pero, señor, por favor…*"

Bellamy rolled his eyes. Must they always plead for their lives? Was it not better to walk silently and with dignity? "Keep the corpse chained for *dead* weight," he instructed his crew.

"HA!" Knox pulled the prisoner from the line and dragged him, attached to the dead seaman, to the gape where the wooden plank jutted over the sea. Knox pressed his cutlass to the shivering man's back as he shuffled him toward the edge. "Any last words?"

The man closed his eyes. *"En el nombre del Padre, y del Hijo, y del Espíritu Santo…"*

Knox pushed him off before he could finish his trinity prayer. A loud splash sounded below. Bellamy loved the commotion more than he cared to admit.

"Green stars approach!" Newell called, Bellamy's first mate's favorite expression for the hungry sparkle in a crocodiles' eyes. Tossing bodies overboard had attracted reptiles of the brackish waters before, thus they arrived quickly.

"Next!" Bellamy ordered.

One by one, he watched the lineup disappear punctuated by a Red Witch at the end of the line, one who would not weep, even as she awaited her fate. Nothing irritated him more than a woman who would not submit.

With shouts of protest, the men shuffled back on their heels, while Knox shoved them off the plank with a kick centered on their backs when they would not jump willingly.

The prisoners plunged toward the eager reptiles, happy for the rare delicacies. One by one, they ripped their flesh to pieces, much to the captain's delight. *See now, those are grateful creatures,* he thought.

Soon, the feeding frenzy had turned the orange waters deep purple. Fourteen became thirteen—became three, two, then one. Finally, as promised, the enemy captain's sorceress wife was the last to walk.

She stood still as a marble statue at the plank's edge, chin lifted high in resolute pride. Her blood-stained green dress wavered in the salty breeze, and for but one moment, the captain considered keeping her for himself to distract him from long nights.

But no—women aboard vessels, they be bad luck, and she had already proven this to be true. Rogue storms did not appear out of nowhere to sink loads of gold amid calm waters. She had been *Córdoba*'s downfall from the beginning—not the *Vanquish*—and he could not allow her to become his as well.

"Prepare to join your husband," Bellamy said, taking slow steps toward her. This fall he wished to watch from a better vantage point. "Any last words before becoming a croc's sweet ending course?"

The ginger wench stared at the horizon and quarter moon, a peaceful expression across her cheeks. She turned a rebellious gaze on him that filled him with momentary dread. "To all who sail this ship, may the waning moon's light condemn you to an eternity of grief and pain..."

Bloody hell? Was this blasted woman actually delivering a curse on his very deck?

"Get rid of her!" Bellamy shouted, a shiver of repressed fear running through his veins.

The woman went on, as Bellamy's crew paused in rapt attention. "...forever to wander, marooned on land between life and death. You will never know peace again. So mote it be..."

Seeing no one exterminating the wench, the captain lunged at her, determined to push her off himself, but the woman stepped off the plank and plunged into the seas on her own terms, irons dragging her to the sandy bottom. When one crocodile moved upon her then floated belly-up, the captain knew he was doomed.

Bellamy watched the rest of the crocs retreat and the woman's body sink, her last breath rising as bubbles to the surface before exploding like dying stars. As

Moses' staff turned the Nile to blood, each of her bubbles ruptured into black tendrils spreading toward his ship.

Vanquish's men gasped and scattered to hide.

Bellamy stared into the water. "A demon be upon us..."

The poisoned mist whirled toward him and the waters receded, exposing a jagged seabed, as if the Devil himself had taken a deep breath before exhaling. Low on the horizon, a wide green mist tumbled toward them, bringing lightning and rumbling dark clouds.

"Rogue wave!" the watch shouted.

The seabed trembled. A folding wave of green water rose then raced towards them.

This was it...

"Lash yourselves!" Bellamy ordered. Never had he imagined waking upon calm waters this morning, that he would be condemned to a watery death by a wicked woman.

The crew scattered for rope and threw themselves against the rails. They tied the rope tightly and prayed to the last. Some men abandoned ship, but Bellamy would not leave the *Vanquish*. He lashed himself to the helm and held his arms wide at the inbound wave, challenging it to take him.

The wave struck mid-ship, lifted *Vanquish* high on its peak, tossing her inland where ravenous crocs, serpents, and God knew what other swamp creatures awaited to feast on them. Bellamy knew how to sail the ocean, not a river of grass. The very idea of wild lands frightened him.

The grasses would serve as a prison from which the ship would never escape.

Vanquish rolled from keel to deck, pushed ten leagues north of the bay deep into the marshland. Her masts and bulkheads crumpled and snapped like bones in a wolf's maw. All of Bellamy's crew drowned or were crushed, slashed to bits through the sawgrass and coquina crags.

As for the captain himself, the green mist rose and enveloped him, as he cast his last words into the night. "This be witch's work. Nigh be time to die."

TWO

Present Day

"And that, ladies and gentlemen, is the tale of the legendary pirate ship doomed to roam the Florida Everglades forever."

The setting sun cast its perfect palette of orange and purple shadows over the sawgrass seas, and my work day was done.

"I hope you've enjoyed my airboat tour of the River of Grass. Any questions?"

A small child of about seven raised his hand high in the air. "Is that a gator tooth on your necklace?"

I pinched the charm between my fingertips. "Yes, you like it?"

He nodded. "Is it from the crocodile that ate the people?"

"No," I laughed, leaning into the boy. "That was just a spooky story I told."

A spark of curiosity twinkled in his eyes. "But can we see the pirate ship?"

"You mean, does it still exist?" I asked. He must not have understood that my tale was a famous Everglades *legend.*

He nodded, his proud parents taking pics and videos

14

behind him.

I crouched, looking at the boy straight in his dark brown eyes. "What's your name?"

"Nathan."

"Well, Nathan. They say that on dark nights when the moon is only a sliver, you can still see the doomed ship sailing along, searching for a way out, its ghostly crew trapped in a prison of watery grass."

"The River of Grass." The kid parroted the nickname I'd used throughout my tour. Most tourists mistakenly thought the Everglades were a stagnant swamp, but I always made sure to clarify that it was a wide, slow-moving river. It overflowed from Lake Okeechobee then headed south until it emptied into Florida Bay.

"You were paying attention. I like that." I smiled.

"Are there other ghosts out there?" Nathan's mouth parted ever so slightly, hesitation at his lips. His parents' enthusiasm dampened slightly.

I could have told him no. Or that my tribe didn't dabble in the paranormal so I wasn't sure, or that because of my culture and religion, I wasn't supposed to speak of such things. But I knew ghosts were real—I'd seen them.

I didn't want to lie to the boy. "Some people say there are," I answered carefully.

"Have *you* seen them?" he asked.

Everyone in the airboat, not just Nathan or his parents, watched me, hinged on my reply. Nineteen people stared at this thirty-one-year-old Miccosukee woman, and I knew what they wanted. They wanted thrill. Entertainment. It was why they had paid for my airboat ride, besides to learn about the *Kahayatle's* ecosystem. They wanted a good time, a story they could post to their Instagrams.

I nodded. "I have."

Maybe not the pirate ship, per se. But I'd seen spirits. My little brother's, for instance—the day he passed away—but that was one ghost tale I would never tell again. Not to anyone.

Nathan leaned back to sink into his mother's arms, as she whispered that it was just a story, nothing to worry about. A shadow of blame cast over her steely-eyed gaze at me.

I left it at that—didn't want to spook the child anymore than he already was. But the Everglades were most definitely filled with the spirits of many who'd refused to move on. Most nights when I sat outside, quietly meditating over our camp, I could feel them, see their silhouettes in my mind's eye. Lost souls crawling their way out of forgotten memories, begging to be acknowledged, wishing to walk again.

Pushing the thought from my mind, I navigated the airboat back to the Miccosukee Indian Village, our camp out on Tamiami Trail thirty miles west of Miami. The village was a roadside stop where people could get to know our culture, watch alligator wrestling, or buy colorful necklaces made by one of my tribe members. Tomorrow was Gale's turn to do airboat tours, while I'd sit with my grandmother to make beaded craft parrots and gators.

Day after day.

Sun up, sun down.

Make fry bread, beaded animals, put in hours at the daycare, give airboat rides to tourists. Sometimes my life felt like an endless cycle of rote existence, like a residual haunting caught in a replay.

I enjoyed my life—it wasn't that I didn't. But I was past thirty and not much had yet happened. Our family was traditional, so we wore traditional clothes, ate traditional foods, and lived in a traditional way, in our camp instead of in the city like many of my cousins who'd distanced themselves from the camp lifestyle. We weren't as hardcore as the traditional Miccosukee who refused to live on the reservation, though. To them, we were sell-outs.

It wasn't true.

All of us on the reservation were committed to preserving Miccosukee culture. As my uncle had told me a million times: with every passing year, our way of life was disappearing. It was up to us to maintain it. Forget the modern world and focus on our established ways, otherwise one day, all six hundred of us would become three hundred, and three hundred would become one hundred. Before we knew it, the Miccosukee Tribe of South Florida might become another extinct culture. Our blood would continue, the *Kahayatle* would continue, but our lifestyle would perish.

It made me sad to think, but it also left me longing for more.

What if I didn't want to live this way, day in, day out? What if I wanted to move to the city, buy a nice car or big house like many of my cousins? The casino down the road made enough so I wouldn't have to give airboat rides if I didn't want to, but that wasn't the point. The point of the shows, the tours, the festival every year after Christmas Day was to share our art, music, and activities with the world. So they wouldn't forget. So they'd know we were here and continued to be.

To leave our mark.

I did my part to keep things going, but every time my boat arrived back at the dock, and my tour group hopped out, and some of them handed me dollar tips like they did now, and they took their selfies and returned back to the parking lots…sometimes I wished I could go with them.

Get me out of this place, my heart would scream. *I want to see the world.*

I reminded myself that the grass was not greener on the other side. Lots of people with complicated lifestyles wished they could live in a simpler way like mine, telling spooky stories on the airboat, enjoying the sunshine, a life with few bills to pay, pointing out flora and fauna before returning to the village to discuss the day with family. I'd remind myself that life was good, even if I didn't whole-heartedly feel it.

Still, I wanted to feel it.

"*Gracias. Muy amable,*" I told a woman who made her teen daughter give me a five-dollar bill. I had heard them speaking "Spanglish" during the tour. "Thank you. Thank you so much." The last family handed me two crumpled dollar bills for my two hours of carefully disseminated information.

Good thing I didn't depend on these tips. I cringed to think how others survived in the modern world on these meager earnings. "Drive safe. Careful with those speed bumps."

The white family turned their faces over the shoulders to giggle at my joke. On the tour, I'd mentioned moving speed bumps, otherwise known as alligators sunning in the middle of Highway 41.

"Thanks for the great tour. What was your name again?"

I turned around.

Two of my tour passengers—a man and a woman—stepped up to me. They were a couple, judging from the way the woman had her arm slinked through her boyfriend or husband's the entire tour like her life depended on him.

"I'm Avila Cypress," I said, shaking the man's hand.

"Pretty name." The woman tapped it into her phone.

She was fair-skinned with luxurious long black hair pulled into a thick ponytail. Her nails were painted a bright blue to match the hull of the boat, and her khaki shorts, green polo, and white visor told me she'd carefully planned this as her "Florida Adventure" outfit.

"Avila," she said. "I am going to write a review online of that presentation because it was just that wonderful. Thank you so much."

"Oh. I'm so glad you enjoyed it." I was relieved. I never knew how people would react to the airboat rides. Generally speaking, people found them to be either extremely interesting if they loved nature, or extremely boring. Hence why I added the spooky tales. Throw a little excitement in there.

"We did," the man said, a handsome black guy in his forties, I would guess. "In fact, we're familiar with all those legends and ghost tales you talked about. We heard about your tour and were hoping you'd mention Villegas House."

My ears burned.

A tremor shuddered in my chest.

How did they know about Villegas House? Very little was written about the dilapidated old depot out in Big Cypress that'd once belonged to a famous environmentalist. They must've read about it on that crappy *Deadly Florida* website that'd been circulating the internet a few years now, because as far as I knew, only locals knew about Villegas House, and God knew, it was taboo to even discuss it.

"Was it something we said?" The man cocked his head.

"Sorry." I blinked. "It's just, nobody ever mentions

that house."

"Ah." The man reached into his pocket and handed me a twenty-dollar bill. "Well, we're Kane and Eve Parker. This is for today's tour, but we were hoping you'd be available to give us a private tour of Villegas House in your free time. It has a reputation for being haunted."

"Yes, I know. That's why I didn't mention it." And it would take a lot more than a twenty to get me to even consider going to that place.

"Why? It fits right in with your other ghost tales." Kane cocked an eyebrow. "Doesn't it?"

"No, it doesn't." I folded the twenty and slid it into my bag. "Villegas House is an actual place with actual history, not good history either. It's not a campfire tale, Mr. Parker. Besides being haunted, it's a rotting death trap. No one in their right minds would go there."

"Well, you see…that's just it." Kane looked at his wife and chuckled. "We're not in our right minds." He adjusted his baseball cap. A flashy Rolex told me that twenty-dollar bill was chump change to him. "We're interested in seeing it and were told you're the only one who knows where it is."

"Who told you that?" My eyebrows knit together.

It wasn't true. Many of us knew about it. We just never mentioned it.

"Sources." Kane smiled a row of perfect teeth.

The only person I knew, besides me, who had a fascination with Villegas House was John, our airboat tours manager, so much that he'd gotten in trouble with my uncle once for mentioning it to tourists. Miccosukee folks avoided the place like the plague. Not only were we traditional but also Christian, so venturing into a haunted, condemned house was not our idea of a good time.

And so, we stayed pretty much silent on the topic.

But that didn't stop me from thinking about it. Or having nightmares about the place since I was a kid. In them, I'd see them lying all over the forest floor. *The bodies...*

"Hello?" Eve peered into my lost gaze.

I looked at them again. "I'm sorry. Nobody in my camp would ever set foot in that house, and nobody has gone out that way in years."

"Does anyone else, besides you, know where it is?" he asked.

"No," I lied.

Uncle Bob knew, John knew...I was pretty sure at least ten people in my camp knew. I only knew because of my dreams. In them, I'd follow the river upstream to Big Cypress, turn right into a dense cypress island, then end up smack in front of the old two-story, hand-built home.

"Maybe the Miami-Dade Police Department?" I added. "They might have records of the place. Because of what happened there."

"Something about murders?" Mr. Parker asked.

"I'm not at liberty to discuss it."

"Avila, we would so appreciate it if you could show us where it is," Eve said.

I shook my head. "You don't get it. The place is dangerous. It's falling apart. It's a huge liability. I could go on and on."

"We'll sign forms," Mr. Parker said. "Releasing you and the tribe. No worries there."

I sucked in an impatient breath. "It doesn't matter how interested you are in that house, it's bad news. Besides, it's in the middle of a delicate ecosystem that's been undisturbed for fifty years. You'd get eaten by mosquitoes, not to mention pythons who snack on alligators."

I employed all the monsters I could think of to keep them away.

"The spirits there aren't the happy kind either," I added. "They don't want to move on to the other side, they don't care how peaceful the Light is, and trust me, they don't believe in God."

A stare-down took place between the Parkers and me. Something told me they weren't going to back down. They were used to this sort of thing, and my words meant zero to them. One way or another, they would get their wish.

"Perfect. Exactly what we're looking for." His charming smile unnerved me, and I envied his determination. If only I had the courage to insist on the things I wanted the way Mr. Parker did. "Alright, I get it…"

I watched as he reached into his pocket and pulled out his wallet. Hundred-dollar bills shuffled out. Two, then three, then five, then a few more, all in the palm of his hand. With a smooth motion, he folded the money between his fingers and held it up. Tangerine-tinted bills flashed in the light of the sunset. "Would a grand make it worth your time?"

Good Lord, this man.

"I wasn't quiet because I wanted money. I was quiet because I can't take you. End of story." Part of me hated the fact he was trying to tempt me with money and another part of me…hated myself for saying no.

The truth was, I itched to see Villegas House for myself. I could face it once and for all. Get it out of my system. Shelf that obsession away forever.

A thousand bucks right there in his hand, but that wasn't the possibility that buzzed in my ears. It was opportunity—to see something new, to finally meet the old creepy house, to hang with new people, for once. It didn't have to take long. All I had to do was airboat them out, show them the error of their ways, and call it a night. Show myself there was nothing to be scared of, then go home.

Speaking of home, it was getting dark out, and tonight was my turn to make dinner. "I appreciate the offer, but I can't. I'm headed home now. Thank you for the gratuity." I smiled and moved past them, bustling toward the rental shop before I changed my mind.

From the slow crunch of gravel, I could tell they were casually following me. "We're staying at the resort and casino," Eve called out. "We'll be here 'til Monday. If you change your mind, just give us a call."

Kane and Eve Parker were different from other families on the boat—more put-together, polished, rehearsed. They'd done this before.

I faced them. "Thank you both for the offer. But I can't take you. It wouldn't be right. I'd be in hot water with my tribe."

Mr. Parker's gaze connected with mine again, as though sending silent messages to try and alter my decision. His wife handed me a business card— ShadowBox Productions with an old-style television set for a logo.

"I think I've insulted you, Ms. Cypress." He reached into his wallet and pulled out more hundreds. "Two thousand. Your time and trouble is worth more than my original offer. I apologize."

I stared at the bills in his hand. They really wanted to see this house, didn't they?

THREE

Worse than staring at two thousand dollars was someone *watching* you stare at two thousand dollars. Kane and Eve Parker clearly didn't realize that I didn't need their financial assistance, but I may as well have been a hungry dog salivating over a nice, juicy steak from the way I stood there, staring at the money.

The casino profits gave us more than enough. We lived modestly and worked at the camp every day, but make no mistake—we were set for life. This wasn't about money. This was about me selling out to a different lifestyle, something my family would frown upon and would send our most traditional members into a moral tizzy.

"Only one day." Kane Parker raised an eyebrow.

The "what ifs" snuck into my mind again. What if I wanted a career? What if I didn't want to live this way anymore? Kane Parker may as well have been holding a ticket to freedom in his hand.

"Your call," he said. "We do a show on Netflix called *Haunted Southland*. Maybe you've heard of it?"

Haunted Southland? I watched it all the time. Was that where they were from?

The host was an older woman with a deep Southern

accent named Sharon Roswell from Atlanta, Georgia. Their investigations were always at the coolest homes and cemeteries, and I always felt a pang of envy when they explored these beautiful locations. Their equipment was modern, and I appreciated the way they respected the spirit world. Most of the time. Sometimes, Sharon could push the envelope to try and get the spirits riled up.

I nodded. "I've watched a few episodes."

Parker's face lit up. "Yeah? Nice. Well, we've explored all the antebellum plantations, haunted gardens, and battlefields we're ever going to see, and this time, we were hoping to shoot a unique Southern location for once. Somewhere exotic. That was when one of our staff mentioned Villegas House in the Everglades."

Exotic was not the world I would have chosen to describe Villegas House's crumbling structure. "It *would* make a cool episode. Too bad I can't take you."

He smirked and withdrew the bills, pressing them back into his wallet. "It *is* too bad. We were hoping, if we liked you, maybe you'd like to join us on a few more shoots. Go on a few expeditions with us. Our ghost consultant is about to retire."

Ghost consultant.

They were scouting me to possibly hire me.

While it was nice that someone finally appreciated my talents and was willing to pay me for it, at the end of the day, being a "ghost consultant," if that was such a thing, wasn't who I was. Watching ghost shows in secret was who I was. I enjoyed learning about the paranormal from afar. And that was the way it had to be if I wanted to avoid dishonoring my family.

"I truly appreciate it, but hopefully you'll understand."

Mr. Parker and his wife exchanged quiet looks. "Then, we're sorry to have taken your time. Thank you so much for the tour. It was entertaining, definitely a pleasure." He tipped his hat and tacked on that wide smile again.

"The pleasure was mine. Thank you for visiting the Miccosukee Village."

That's it, Avila. Walk away. Your ancestors would be proud.

"Again, if you change your mind, we'll be at the hotel and casino a few more days," Mrs. Parker called out. "The number on the card is my direct line."

"Got it," I said, holding the card up in the air. I wondered if they would continue their hunt for a tour guide, or if they'd go home empty-handed now that I'd turned them down. My guess was they'd somehow make it to Villegas House anyway—they'd just find someone else to take them. Deep down, I hated that.

I trudged toward the rental office. Entering the chickee and heading toward John, I waited until the Parkers had driven off in their Rove Ranger before tossing their card in the trash bin and letting go of the biggest exhale ever.

"What's up?" John shuffled through a stack of envelopes. "More customers who think the sawgrass wasn't exciting?"

"Nah, they were fine," I replied. I wasn't about to share what had just happened with John in front of Charlie Cypress, eavesdropping from the back office. The man was good friends with the General Council's Assistant Chairman—a.k.a. my uncle. He would only tell me I'd done the right thing by turning them down, and I wasn't so sure.

John handed me my paycheck. "Have a good weekend, Avila. Say hello to your mom and *pooshe* for me."

"I will." I ripped open my envelope and stared at the

meager earnings that were more a token than a salary. For a moment, I entertained the idea of waving down the Parkers' truck. I wanted to see the house that had haunted me my whole life, the crumbling structure I had dreamed about, the place of terrible stories I'd heard.

The location of my grandfather's death.

That was the main reason nobody spoke about Villegas House. The land was sacred, the final resting place of our head of council—Robert Cypress. Villegas House terrified me so deep in my bones, I never mentioned it for fear that it would come for me just by using its name.

But I didn't chase after Kane and Eve Parker.

I went back to the garbage bin and pulled out the ShadowBox business card. Then, I climbed into my truck and went home.

Just like I did—day in, day out.

After a shower, I went about preparing dinner, grilling bass, and setting the table. My mother looked up from her chair where she sat sewing a new patchwork skirt of blue, red, yellow, white and black. "Set the table for four, Avila."

"Uncle Bob?"

"Yes."

Inwardly, I groaned. Why did Uncle Bob have to come tonight of all nights? It was bad enough I was still reeling from having turned down a once-in-a-lifetime opportunity. I didn't need tradition shoved down my throat, too.

Pooshe strolled into the kitchen to help me flip the fish in the pan, as though I were a child incapable of doing it myself. In *elaponke*, she told me how her own mother used to prepare and cook deer, but never while on her monthly period, as it was considered a sacred act.

I listened politely but my thoughts wandered as she talked. I'd heard all these stories before. She recounted them so I could pass them on to my own kids one day, but that would never happen if I didn't get out of this place and meet someone.

Uncle Bob arrived right on time—as usual.

"*Eelechko*," my mother greeted.

"*Chehuntamo*." Uncle Bob sat at the table, ready for his meal, legs apart, elbows wide. "And there she is…" Something about the way he looked at me made me nervous. My stomach hurt without even knowing why. "Avila Cypress, wannabe ghost hunter."

"What do you mean?" My stomach sank. Why did he have to do this in front of my mother and grandmother?

"We received another complaint about your tour today." He chugged his water and set it down again.

"What?" I stared at him. "About what?"

"About the extra garbage you add to your tours. Spirits? Pirate ships? Avila, you're scaring children now, and people don't sign up for a haunted storytelling hour that has nothing to do with the Everglades. Take them out, show them alligators, tell our history, talk about genocide that must never happen again. Return home. End of story. Can't you do that?"

"I *do* do that," I muttered. Great, another Avila-does-everything-wrong dinner. I was thirty-one and still listening to this crap. "Look, I only add a few mysteries here and there to spice the tour up. People like it when I say the weird tales. It's not hurting anybody."

"Yes, it's hurting us," my mother chimed in. "It's not who we are. When people pay for an airboat ride, they're expecting animals, scenery, photos, history, Miccosukee traditions. Not ghosts."

Uncle Bob gave me a stern look. "That's right. We expect you to tell them about how life is changing. We can't drink the *Kahayatle's* water anymore. Crucial elements of our life are no longer possible. We're fighting to keep these traditions alive. We don't expect you to talk about plane crash victims."

"Flight 411 was an actual event. It's history," I countered. "Maybe not the history you want me to talk about, but history of the Everglades nonetheless. You want me to stop that too?"

"Avila..." My mother eyed me.

"Fine, I'm sorry."

I knew I sounded childlike, but this was only the second time someone had complained, which was unfair, because people complained about the airboat rides no matter what. *They're boring, we didn't see enough, I only saw one alligator...* At least my airboat rides were entertaining. Because of me, we had a 4.5 star rating on TripAdvisor.

"We need you to stick to the script, Avila." Uncle Bob's forehead crinkles warned me not to challenge him. He was my elder. My job was to listen, respect, and promote our ways proudly. As part of the General Council, his was to tell me what to do.

"Avila, we have talked about this." My mother set down her needlework and sat at the table. "You know very well how I feel about all those shows you watch. Ghost this, ghost that. You're inviting dark spirits into your life every time you watch that."

"Really, Mom? By watching TV? Look, I'm not inviting dark spirits in. I'm not playing with a Ouija board or anything. I'm not into the occult, if that's what you think. If I mention ghosts in my tours, it's only for entertainment value. I'll stop, okay?"

"You will," my uncle said. "Or we'll leave the airboat

tours to Gale."

"You don't need to do that." I gritted my teeth then slapped on a fake, grateful smile. I liked the airboat rides. I liked the peacefulness and the fact it was the only way I got to interact with people outside our camp. "Now, can we eat?"

Stick to the script. Smile and accept the tips.

Got it.

From the time I was little, we were encouraged to learn traditional ways but also non-Indian ways as well. It was the reason we went to private schools who employed all kinds of people from all different races and backgrounds, so we could harmonize with the outside world, not be isolated from it. Well, guess what? The outside world held a fascination with the supernatural, and so did I.

"We just don't want you misrepresenting our culture," my uncle added, as my grandmother silently set the fish and fry bread on the table. We gave thanks to God for this bounty and ate in silence.

I had nothing else to say, nothing to add. More than ever, I wanted out of there, to drive down the road to my cousin Kellie's in Miami and watch movies, to get away for a while. We might even watch *Haunted Southland* on Netflix, now that I'd personally met the producers. I could tell her about the money I was offered without getting an earful. I could be myself without feeling like I was being judged and that "me" was a mix of tradition and modern ways.

After dinner and cleanup, I sat in my room and picked up the faded photo of my grandfather. Long hair pulled into a ponytail, crinkly eyes, handsome smile, wearing the same gator tooth necklace I now wore. Having died long before I was born, I'd never met him but always felt close. When I was little, I'd get into trouble, pick up this photo, and imagine myself talking to him, telling him my woes. He'd always tell me to hang in there and fight another day.

Next to it was the card Eve Parker had handed me— ShadowBox Productions.

Being around a TV crew might be good for me. God forbid I should learn a new skill. Hiring me as a consultant would mean getting to travel around the country, investigate cases, and I got goose bumps just thinking about it.

Yes, I respected my family and tribe, but what about me?

I needed to live my own life.

My little brother had died on the side of US-41 at the age of six in a truck crash we'd been involved in. Minutes before, he'd asked me if he could ride in the front for once, and I'd switched places with him while Mom drove. He'd been the same age as that little boy on the boat today.

He'd died so that I could live.

That terrible night, I watched a wispy white light rise out of his chest and disappear into the ceiling only moments after he'd drawn his last breath. About a year later, he visited me while I was in bed. Scared the living shit out of me. Appeared as a filmy gray apparition by my bedside. I never got to talk to him, because lurking behind him had been an ominous, dark energy.

Immediately, I began praying to make him go away.

He did. So did the cloudy darkness.

I'd been praying for them to stay away every night ever since.

Billie never had the chance to do more with his life. Neither had the passengers of Flight 401 who perished out in the Everglades. Neither did any of the people killed and made to "disappear" out in the *Kahayatle*. But I did. And I'd never shake the guilt of surviving either. I carried it with me like a cross.

My mind whirled with the possibilities. For the first time in a long time, I felt like there could be more for me.

I waited until my mother was asleep before calling the casino resort and leaving a message for Kane and Eve Parker to call me in the morning. I said my prayers, told my brother I loved him like I did every night, and fell into a dreamless, peaceful sleep.

FOUR

Sunrise over the Everglades was the most beautiful thing about living here. I didn't see the early morning sight often enough. Today, though, as I waited by the side of the access road that would lead us deep into Big Cypress National Preserve, I soaked it all in—the golden rays filtering through the cypress trees, the reflection of blue sky over the water, the anhinga quietly perched on a log, spreading his wings to dry.

So much magnificence and stillness.

Yet ShadowBox Productions wanted to see the ugly parts.

I'd taken the offer. Two weeks ago, I'd spoken to Eve and told her I'd escort them out to Villegas House after all, but they could not mention it to the tribe. She couldn't have been more delighted that I'd changed my mind, and the more we talked over the phone, the more I liked her and felt this would be an exciting opportunity for me, especially if they were considering keeping me on for other projects.

Eve told me they'd return to their home base in Atlanta, plan the Everglades episode, then come back to South Florida in two weeks with the crew. That should give me enough time to prepare.

For two weeks, I thought about how to tell my family that I wouldn't be home for a day, possibly two, because I'd taken a tour job to Villegas House. In the end, there was no good way to do that. For the first time in my adult life, I'd lied straight to my mother's face. I'd told her I was going fishing with Kellie, and though my mom had thought that was strange, she'd shrugged and told me to have a good time.

That might've made me a liar, but I couldn't do it.

Especially after the talking-to I'd been given during dinner that evening, which only reinforced why I felt stuck. Perhaps if I ended up with a job consulting haunted places for the production crew, they might be proud of me and understand why I had to do it. But I had to tell them eventually. I wouldn't be able to live in good conscience otherwise.

Taking in the last few moments while waiting for the crew to arrive, I thought about what might happen at Villegas House. The place was built in the 50s by Roscoe Nesbitt, the father of the two gladesmen brothers who taunted the new residents there in 1967. I knew this because I'd overheard my uncle talking about it to councilmen when I was a kid, though nobody was supposed to know what happened there.

I know that Gregory H. Rutherford, an English environmentalist and avian expert, moved into the deep Everglades cabin a decade after Roscoe moved out and claimed it was uninhabitable due to its haunted nature. The place served as his home and rescue center where he, his Cuban wife, Elena Villegas, and two biologists all lived, studying the natural habitat and rehabilitating injured animals.

As soon as he moved in, bad stuff started happening.

William and Richard Nesbitt began coming around

telling Rutherford and his crew to leave; it was their father's house, even though no permits had officially been pulled to build it. They got into arguments that lasted a couple of years. Besides quarreling over the property, they argued over hunting. Rutherford opposed the shooting of some of the most endangered species in the Everglades—panthers and snail kite—and the Nesbitts argued it was their right to hunt.

I'd always understood both points of view.

What happened next depended on who told the story. I'd spent years trying to decipher the truth. So far, the truth had eluded me, but the gist was this—the Nesbitt brothers went berserk and killed everyone during an argument, including my grandfather. Knowing they'd never get away with murdering a high profile scientist or leader of the Miccosukee Tribe, they killed themselves.

Seven people in total.

Down US-41, the caravan approached. They came in two vans, one of them hauling an airboat. I wasn't sure where they'd rented it, but I hoped it was one of the newer models I felt comfortable driving, since they were pretty tricky to handle, especially in marshy Big Cypress.

A ball of nerves coalesced in my stomach, as I watched the caravan slow down upon seeing me standing by the side of the road, waving my arms. This was it. They were here, and soon, we'd drive up the access road until we couldn't drive anymore. Soon, we'd switch from van to airboat to make our way up the River of Grass. I was crazy—pure crazy to do this. I could already visualize something bad happening and my mom telling me, *en maheem*—I brought it upon myself.

Still, I couldn't wait.

The vans slowed, tires crunching over gravel. They came to a full stop, as new people began stepping out, including the Parkers. The group looked out of place, and I suddenly felt guilty bringing strangers into my homeland.

"The crack of dawn, Cypress?" Mr. Parker joked, coming over to shake my hand with that big smile he wielded so well.

"It's a long journey to where we're going, Mr. Parker," I said. "Trust me, you don't want to boat when the sun is boiling or in the afternoon when the storms begin. Follow me down the road. We'll put the airboat in the water about a mile north of here."

"Listen, call me Kane. Mr. Parker is my father, and by the way, these are my crew. You already know my lovely wife, Eve. That over there…" He pointed to a tall, gangly white man in his late thirties with sandy brown hair hanging over his eyes who'd begun taking photos. Serious, not very friendly, he would soon be sorry he wore a long-sleeved flannel shirt to the Everglades at the height of the steamy wet season. "That's Quinn, our cameraman. BJ Atkins is our tech."

An overweight white man with cropped black hair and black glasses waved at me out the front seat of Kane's rental. I waved back, feeling bad for how obese the man was given how young he looked. Our airboat needed to be delicately balanced between all weighted persons and objects.

"You know our host, Sharon Roswell." He pointed to the blonde woman I'd seen guiding viewers through crumbling sanatoriums and haunted theaters. She stared at her phone, detached, unaware that Kane was introducing her to me. Then, he pointed to another woman, an elderly lady with light auburn cotton candy hair. "And our ghost consultant, Linda Hutchinson. She prefers the term medium." He chuckled.

"Hello!" Linda waved from the window.

"Nice to meet everyone. I'm Avila Cypress. I do the airboat tours on the reservation. I hope you brought sunscreen and plenty of water. We should get moving."

Tapping the hood of my truck, I quickly climbed in behind the steering wheel, just so I wouldn't have to talk anymore. Though I was used to giving tours, being in front of a real, live production crew for a show I actually watched made me nervous.

As I drove up the access road, I tried to figure out if I was scared for good reason or simply because my family had put the fear in me about the place since I was little. A memory of Uncle Bob chastising John for attempting to visit Villegas House one time came to me.

My father didn't die in vain so we could make a mockery of that spot, Uncle Bob had told him. *It's a burial ground now. No one is to ever step foot there again. Last thing we need are gladesmen breathing down our backs.*

He'd meant we didn't need more confrontation with the area's hunters. The weird thing is, gladesmen and traditional Indians weren't all that different. We both lived in camps, migrated according to the season, rode our airboats, hunted and fished, though many of my tribe refused to eat fish from our mercury-tainted waters. Gladesmen passed their way of life on to their young ones just like we did. Some called them rednecks or Cajuns of South Florida. Some called them sawgrass cowboys.

Gladesmen invented the airboat to navigate the marshlands when the Miccosukee were still using dugout canoes. They existed today in much the same way Miccosukee did—marginally—growing more frustrated with their diminishing existence. I'd never known any personally, but I'd run into them before. Always felt intimidated when I'd seen them in town or passing by on my airboat.

I believed my grandfather had tried going up there to ease tensions, using diplomatic tactics to settle the score between the two groups. But the gladesmen weren't having it and killed Rutherford, his wife, his two assistants, and my grandfather. Murdered in cold blood for no good reason. When county police arrived to investigate, they found *seven* dead. The two gladesmen brothers were dead too, their bodies rotting away, as alligators and turtles lingered in the perimeter.

For some reason, police left without concluding their investigation, and area locals had to come bury the bodies themselves. What lived in Villegas House that made them vacate as quickly as they'd arrived?

My brain tingled with nervous excitement.

As we arrived at the edge of the waterway, I cut off my truck's engine. *Nothing bad is going to happen,* I kept telling myself. Cameras might capture an orb or two, they might get a few words on their ghost voice box, but mostly, the wilderness would provide most of the entertainment. I'd get paid, we'd all go home...no harm done.

The party bustled to unload, drop the boat into the water, and get everything aboard. It was a large airboat used for tours, the kind with two levels of seats—five on the upper, five on the lower, with an area underneath the elevated scaffolding to hold all cargo—cameras, black boxes containing tech stuff, tripods, and backpacks.

As everyone carefully stepped in, my worry stuck to the big dude. I didn't want to offend him, but he was going to have to sit in the middle two seats to keep the boat balanced. An airboat was nothing more than a motorized skiff, flimsy enough to skim the surface and cut through tall grass. Choosing a nice sized wading stick off the ground, I thanked Mother Earth for it then threw it into the boat, pushing it to one side.

Once everything was settled, I passed out life vests and ear protection and then Kane stood, propped one foot up on an empty seat. "Alright, anyone have any questions?"

"What do we do if we sink?" Sharon asked. Everyone laughed nervously, shooting looks at her, as if they knew she'd start acting up.

"You swim for the nearest edge," I said.

All eyes fell on me.

"But you won't sink. You got yourselves a decent airboat here, and I'm a certified operator. Just keep a few things in mind: airboats have no brakes. If I see something coming toward us, I can only release the gas and veer off to the side. That's why I won't be driving fast. Better to take our time. Also, keep your hands inside the boat at all times."

"Because…why?" Quinn asked.

"Because gators." I shifted my gaze to his skeptical face. "They jump."

"Good Lord, what do you mean they jump?" Linda pressed a manicured hand to her chest.

I raised my eyebrows. "I mean, they jump. Out of nowhere, sometimes. See the guard rails? They're your friends. The Everglades are beautiful but don't be tempted to stick your hand in the water. Any other questions?"

Nobody spoke up.

"Alright, Kane, I think we're good."

"Let's do it." Kane clapped once and rubbed his hands together with excitement, like a kid getting ready for a big race.

I sank into my seat, put my ear gear on, and turned on the engine. The airboat roared to life, as a few egrets rose into the air and flew away. My passengers all exchanged excited glances. I felt their exhilaration. Today, everything changed. Today, I conquered old fears.

I allowed myself to take in the moment. Be present. Release all guilt.

The warm morning air, sun on my face, brackish water and sawgrass all calmed me. This was my home turf. I was in my element. In about two hours, we would arrive at Villegas House. I couldn't wait to see it, rotting and all. I had to hand it to Kane and Eve—it was the perfect setting for an episode. As long as we got past the front steps, everything would be just fine.

FIVE

Big Cypress—vast wet wilderness.

Still pristine, still ancient.

One of the only places left in the world where you could drive a buggy or an airboat for days and days and never see another person. Even though these lands were protected as part of the national park system, its inhabitants' lifestyles was protected too—the Miccosukee, the Seminole, the gladesmen—and that made us just as vital to life of this ecosystem. This mosaic of cypress trees was our canvas, and the creatures living here were God's works of art.

I wasn't sure anyone else on the boat saw the watery grasslands the way I did. They probably saw an overgrown wasteland. What they didn't know was just how delicate everything was underneath the surface. Life depending on life, depending on water cycles, and to think of the number of times in history where that delicate balance almost went to shit thanks to government.

As my guests and I delved deeper into the glades, we saw the familiar clusters of cypress trees popping up like domes, an above-ground inversion of the rain-filled basin from which they grew. We saw dollar sunfish and large mouth bass, catfish and yellow bullheads. Flying overhead were wood storks, roseate spoonbills, and egrets. I pointed out the various landscapes, such as prairies, hammocks, pinelands, swamps, and estuaries.

To me, they were beautiful. But studying my passengers, I worried for them.

What would happen when it rained, because it was summer and did every day? I hoped they brought ponchos like I'd suggested, mosquito repellant for their delicate skin, and boots for slogging. I hoped they weren't scared of a little lightning in the afternoons. If they were, this would surely suck for them.

But the women on this expedition wore shorts instead of jeans to protect their legs, and the men wore sandals, because visiting Florida, they must've thought that was the thing to do. I sighed to myself and heard my mother's voice in my head telling me that I failed these people.

The sky became overcast. I pushed the airboat along a little faster so we'd have enough time to settle in before the rains came. I cut through water lilies so fast, pig frogs leaped out of our way. Up the river about thirty or so miles, the cypress trees became more dense. We hit a watery fork in the "road," and I knew I'd see it soon.

And isolated cypress island.

In my dreams, Villegas House always emerged from the fog before the sun had a chance to burn the mist away. I wondered if it would appear the same way today. Right when the trees became denser and the waterway more narrow, I knew we were getting closer. I slowed the skiff so we wouldn't miss it, then turned off the engine altogether.

The airboat's vibration ceased, and then, everything went dead quiet.

Only sounds of crickets and mosquitoes echoed over

the river.

If I didn't know where we were headed, I would've said the air felt peaceful. Tranquil. A religious silence. I was almost sure everyone could hear my heart pounding through their ear protection. Our boat drifted underneath mossy overgrowth.

Kane leaned back from his seat. "What are we doing?"

I took off my ear protection and picked up the stick I'd brought. "Wading." I sank the end into the water and used it to push us through just my ancestors had been doing on dugout canoes for centuries. "We're approaching your beloved destination."

He jerked his head at me and gave me a playful, scorned look, but I hadn't hurt Kane's feelings. The man was happier than a squirrel in a pile of acorns now that we were almost here. Finally, he could gaze upon the legendary house he'd so desperately wanted me to show him, so much that he would offer two thousand dollars and the possibility for more.

Everyone slid off their ear protection and slowly looked around. The cameramen aimed their cameras in the new direction of the tree-lined tunnel. Slowly, we waded down a pathway growing more dense with trees and hanging moss. Spiky palmettos stretched across the marsh, reaching to scratch us like jagged fingernails. Kane stood, took a bowie knife off his belt, and cut the longest fronds to get them out of our way.

I bet he'd been waiting all his life to use that knife.

The closer we moved toward our destination, the quieter things became. A sense of foreboding sifted through the sawgrass, like the land itself was waking from a long night of unsettling slumber, sighing at our presence. Nobody dared move or say anything. Only the clicks of the camera shutters broke the silence. Linda occasionally bat at her legs, slapping at mosquitoes, and Sharon bounced her knee nervously, as she sat staring at the right bank, waiting for the house to come into view.

Finally, a dark mass inched through the morning mist, peeking through the foliage like a giant-sized human prisoner crouched in a corner, wasting away, simpering, wondering if his punishment was yet over. Riddled with holes, broken timbers, a sagging wooden roof, and busted windows, half of which were missing, the house seemed ashamed to see us. It front door yawned open like the last person to leave knew nobody would ever return to chastise them. The horizontal planks of the house were dark brown to black, covered in patches of bright green moss in some spots, in others penetrated with rogue, swirling vines. Jesus—it looked as though the earth itself was a python slowly unhinging its fangs and swallowing the thing back up.

In the pit of my stomach, a knot tightened. It was too late to turn back.

I pulled the airboat as close as I could to the island, but there was no shore on which to bank. There were cypress trees and palmetto trees and thick mangrove roots we had to navigate before stepping onto firm land, hence the slogging we were about to do.

"Is that as close as you can get?" Sharon glanced at me over her shoulder.

I cast side-eye at her. I wasn't the only one. I definitely saw a few eyerolls from the rest of the crew. "Yes, ma'am. Until this boat grows legs anyway," I said.

I hadn't meant for it to sound snippy, but for a woman who hadn't said two words to me since she arrived, she could've asked more politely. I knew, though, that tensions were high now that we were here.

I turned to Kane. "This part is tricky. There's no definition between water and land, so we're just going to have to slog."

"What does that mean?" Sharon asked, sharp blue eyes accusing me. "Slog?"

"Roswell, remember in the meeting, I told you all to bring boots?" Kane asked, nodding. "Well, it was for this. I just didn't know we needed them now."

"Yes, you need them now," I said. I should've asked them to change shoes while still on land, but I wasn't used to leading a slogging experience.

"Let's go, guys. Get them on."

"Move slowly, please!" I called out, so everyone wouldn't move at once. Smartly, BJ let everyone shift about the boat first while he stayed anchored in the middle.

"You want us to go in the water?" Sharon asked calmly.

"It's the only way to get to the house," I said. "There's no dock here. It's not deep. You just wade a few steps until you get to the bank, then you climb over the roots."

"You say that like this isn't Florida."

She was making it a big deal by not trusting me, but I supposed this could look pretty intimidating to anyone who'd never done it before.

"What if there's gators or snakes?" she asked.

"There could be, but you all wanted to come here, not me," I mumbled under my breath. Most heard me and gave me wary glances. Kane and Eve gave each other silent looks.

"Great spot, guys," Quinn said sarcastically, getting on his boots.

"Alright, look, don't worry," I added. "We're going to

move quickly, and if there was a gator, you would see it coming. The water is crystal clear, see?" I gestured to the water that was, in fact, pretty darn beautiful for being marshland. People thought swamp water was mucky or putrid, but it was absolutely vibrant, since it was actually a river.

"Everyone grab what they can," Eve ordered. "So we only have to do this once."

One by one, the production crew got their proper shoes on, dropped into the water up to their knees, and pulled off bags from the skiff. Hoisting boxes over their shoulders, onto their backs, they handed them to each other and worked like a team.

BJ looked at me for permission. "Go ahead," I told him. A captain never abandoned their ship until they were the last, so I stayed onboard and kept an eye on the water in case any curious moccasins decided to swim by right as BJ struggled to disembark.

Only when everyone had pulled themselves onto firm cypress island did I jump into the water with the remaining bags and wade toward the island as well. Climbing up using the walking stick, I bent to catch my breath. "You all might want to find a stick, too. They come in handy." Facing the house, I gestured and my hands fell by my sides. "And there you have it—Villegas House."

Except for the occasional "damn" or "holy shit" muttered under their breaths, the group hushed to study the decrepit old cabin. I called it a cabin, though it was really a large, two-story house built crudely without permits. Rotten and even more decayed the closer we got, the house just felt...forsaken.

I shouldn't have come here.

I shouldn't have brought these people.

If my tribe had asked us all to stay away, there had to be a reason.

No, Avila. It's fine. It's just old.

As Quinn and BJ took photos, Sharon stood taking it all in, and Eve stuck tightly to Kane's side. They soaked in the monstrosity they'd asked to see.

"We've seen some crazy shit, guys," Kane said. "But this is the craziest ever."

"So true, baby," Eve said, taking photos. "But it's beautiful."

Linda, the medium who'd been standing off to the side quietly, stepped over to me. "It's dark," she said. "Much darker than I imagined."

"Yes, it's the wood," I told her. "Probably Dade pine that's rotted through…"

"No, I mean its aura."

I looked at her. "Excuse me?"

"The house's aura. It's dark, like a gunmetal silver. I don't like it." She stared at the house with narrowed eyes. I could see she felt it was a mistake to come here. If the medium of this expedition was having second thoughts, that didn't fill me with confidence of any kind. She glanced at me. "Your aura is bright, though. Are you spiritual?"

I was a bit taken aback. "Mine?"

"Yes, it's beautiful. Bright blue with a silver lining to it. Do you have psychic gifts?" Her fluffy reddish hair shook, as she tilted her head to examine me from a few more angles. I stood still in case her studying my aura required me to remain motionless.

"Not that I know of."

Yes, I had psychic gifts, but I'd worked too hard to suppress them to have her bringing them out into the open again.

From the day I'd seen Billie's spirit rise, to the day he visited me in my bedroom, to seeing the dark entity hovering behind him, I knew I was psychic to some degree. But like any skill, it could die away from atrophy if uncultivated, and that was exactly what I'd tried to do all my life. I wasn't strong enough to deal with real spirits. I didn't know how people like Linda did it. I didn't mind knowing the ghosts were there, and I loved telling stories about them, as long as they left me alone.

Linda's Mona Lisa smile hinted that she didn't believe me. "Well, you should be," she said. For an old woman, she was beautiful but also seemed to have gone through a lot in her life. Melancholy lingered just inside her eyes, and the laugh lines outside of them seemed to weep.

"What do you mean by the house has an aura?" I asked. "I always thought auras were the fields of energy surrounding *living* things."

Her almond-shaped brown eyes focused on Villegas House. Lips pressed together, she nodded like saying it out loud might make it true. "Exactly."

SIX

A house as a living thing. With its own dark gray aura. *Great.*

The very thought sent a spike of unease through me, but it was too late to leave now. Here we were, and here we'd stay until this job was done or one of us got swallowed by the house's aura, whichever came first.

Calm down.

I was surrounded by people. What could happen surrounded by so many people?

Kane's crew got to setting up tents, opening backpacks, cracking open equipment cases, running cables, and starting a generator. Its rumbling ripped through the tranquility, and I thought of the animals that lived here and what they'd think of us for disturbing their peace. The ghosts, too.

Were they watching us now?

As it turned out, I would be sharing a tent with Linda. Kane and Eve would be taking their own, the two tech guys, Quinn and BJ, were sharing, and Sharon had apparently requested her own tent, which was fine, since her ego needed a big place to sleep. I felt more comfortable sharing with Linda, anyway, even though she didn't seem to want to be here.

Once we'd set up camp, the crew stood facing Villegas House, taking photos and talking about what they'd do once they went in. I realized they weren't entering, not because they were scared to, but because they had an established methodology for doing these investigations. Everything was recorded, so it wasn't until cameras got rolling would Sharon or anyone set foot inside.

I was itching to find out what would be inside the crumbling rotten structure but grateful that the *Haunted Southland* crew would be finding out first. I'd be waiting outside. By the tent. In the safe area.

BJ had set up a couple of monitors which connected signals with their video cameras, so anything that Quinn taped while inside, we could see it out in the "tech tent." They did a test run on lighting, Sharon's voice and movements, and a few other video tests I didn't understand because I didn't speak TV production. Everyone was too busy to explain what they were doing. I liked the buzz of it, however—the energy this team created. They worked cohesively, like a well-oiled machine, and I felt envious of their chemistry.

Mosquitos invaded after noon, so I made myself useful going around, spraying repellant on anyone who would let me. We didn't use repellant in our camp, but anyone not used to mosquitos definitely needed it.

A female presence sidled up to me and spoke in a southern accent. "What can you tell me about this place, Cypress?"

It was Sharon, hands on hips, chin gesturing to the house. She was taller than I was, statuesque, and though she was in her mid-40s, it was easy to see that she had once been a beautiful twenty-something with a career in television. I'd read somewhere that she'd used to be an

NFL cheerleader turned soap actress turned ghost investigator, a smart move if you asked me, because youthful beauty did not live forever.

"Honestly, I don't know much. Only that a gladesman elder built the place in the fifties. He left almost as soon as he finished it. Later on, his sons would get into one altercation or another with an environmentalist who moved in, then one day, there was an accident."

"An accident, or a murder?" She raised an eyebrow.

"Nobody knows for sure. I mean, we know it ended in death, because they came out here to investigate. There's photos online of decomposed corpses lying around, but that's all they have. They didn't stick around long to find many facts."

"Could it have been a natural death? Like an animal attack?"

I shrugged. "I don't know of any creature that would do that. The Everglades has its mysterious Skunk Ape, kind of like a Big Foot, but it's peaceful—if it's real, that is—not something that would kill seven people."

"What about panthers?" Sharon faced me. I could almost envision her as a police officer with uniform, badge, gun in holster and everything.

"Florida panthers are shy. I doubt a panther would've killed everyone that day, especially hunters who would've ended it with one shot."

"Were there any women here?" Sharon asked.

"Women? Um, well, there was Rutherford's wife, Elena. Plus I believe one of the assistants was a woman. Why?"

"Just curious. What about the Nesbitt brothers? Were either married or were their wives part of the confrontation that took place?"

"Thing is, I don't really know. Everything I've learned has been passed down orally, and you know how that is. Details change from year to year." For being considered for ghost consultant, I really didn't know much, did I?

"What happened after the killings?" Sharon asked. "Did anyone come back and experience anything strange? What's the haunted history like?"

Sharon's questions were starting to bother me. Not because I didn't have the answers she wanted, or because she seemed to think I was the Wikipedia of Villegas House, but because she seemed to want them for her own. Kane had told me that we'd have a meeting once we got here, where I'd share all I knew about the house, but Sharon had isolated me and interrogated me. Just a little Avila-Sharon session.

"Ms. Roswell, I know very little about its haunted history," I said, staring at the ground, a mix of grass, sand, but also shards of wood. "I only know that my tribe stays away from here. They consider it bad luck. They've told stories of men who've come back to the village changed, never to be the same after visiting. It's a legend because no one knows what really happened. The Everglades has a habit of blurring the past that way."

Sharon frowned. "I thought you were the hired historian, but you don't know shit."

"I…" I tried not to feel rattled, but my pride was hurt. Who did she think she was? "I'm not an historian. There is no historian about this house. I'm only here because I guess I was the only one naïve enough to bring you."

Sharon's bright blue eyes scanned over my face, as if she could read my intentions and find out if I was lying. She didn't trust me, but that was okay—I didn't trust her either, and I hadn't come here to make friends.

"You were the only one, huh?" She smirked then turned to watch the crew setting up. "Well, we'll have to use Linda as much as we can then. She's the reason I'm here."

I looked at the aging medium sitting in her camping chair outside out tent, doing a crossword puzzle. She stopped, fished the ground for a piece of wood and held it with eyes closed. She seemed underappreciated, as though she saw herself as an older woman of little or no value. Which was sad, because so far, she'd been the only one who'd provided any useful information about Villegas House.

As curious as I was, I didn't want to continue engaging with Sharon any more than I had to. Talk about the real person being completely different from the celebrity. She skulked off to my relief.

I took a seat next to Linda

She handed me the bark. "Look at this. What do you think?"

I took the shard of wood and flipped it over in my hands. It seemed to be from the house, same color, same type of wood, and everything. "Probably a broken piece from the house. Why, what do you think it is?"

"I know it's from the house. That's not what I mean. Close your eyes. Tell me what you feel." She closed her hands around mine with the wood tucked in my palm.

I closed my eyes and felt the wood, its density, the smoothness of its surface. It wasn't Dade pine, and it wasn't Cypress, so it may have been any kind of imported wood from the days when Gregory Rutherford lived out here, but none of that mattered or was why she'd asked me to hold it.

The only thing that mattered was that my chest hurt. Breaths became shallow, as though I'd run a marathon, and my side cramped, yet I couldn't drop the stupid piece of wood.

Its effect had taken a hold of me like an electrical current. I gasped and finally threw the piece of wood on the ground. "What the hell was that?"

Linda nodded, satisfied. She sat back in her chair, as though her suspicions had been right. "You're like me, Avila. You see beyond the veil."

SEVEN

Of course she knew.

She was bloody psychic.

I dragged my gaze away from her, hoping she wouldn't mention it to anybody, but my silence was admission enough.

"Alright, everybody. Over here, let's talk." Kane clapped his hands together once and swung his arms, waiting while everybody made their way to the center of camp. He sat on top of a crate and swung his baseball cap backwards. "We're ready to do this, Avila," he said. "First and foremost, thank you for bringing us here. We know how hard it was for you, but do know that we really appreciate it."

Everyone looked at me. Only Eve and Linda smiled.

"No problem," I said. Actually, big problem. But that was my burden to bear, one I'd deal with when I returned home. I appreciated his acknowledgement, though.

"Also, thank you, Linda. I know it's not always easy for you, doing what you do, but we appreciate you being here, as always."

"I'll be here if you need me, sweetheart," Linda said in a melodious voice. Turning to me, she mumbled, "My work comes later."

"We like to receive impressions without her in the beginning, then bring her in afterwards," Sharon clarified for me, as though Linda's explanation hadn't been enough.

"Yeah, for the heavy lifting." Linda smirked. "Which there will be. I can tell."

Sharon ignored her.

I nodded and focused back on Kane. Next to me, Linda fanned herself with a folder. The woman did not look well, and the heat and humidity were pretty oppressive, even for me.

"Avila, this is for you, since we know it already. Keep everything dry, cell phones off, loose jewelry taped or put away. Like what you've got there..." He pointed to my neck. I instinctively touched my gator tooth necklace. "Not that it looks noisy. In case you're in any of our shots, Sharon's our host, so we don't do, say, or touch anything without her OK. She's the one who guides this whole process onscreen."

A slice of panic cut through me. "I'm going to come out in this?" I thought I was just here for the ride, quietly hiding in the background.

"We don't plan on having you in any scenes, but you never know. Sometimes spirit activity affects the crew in different ways, and people end up on screen."

"Okay." Last thing I needed was to come out on *Haunted Southland* and have my family see me escorting strangers to Villegas House before I was ready to tell them. Though eventually, word would get out that a show had been taped here.

Kane went on about technical things. He may as well have been speaking a different language. "We'll need to boost the gain," he told Quinn and BJ. "Check the batteries, I don't want to break the stream."

"Do we go with a ring light?" Quinn asked. "Or softie?"

"Ring light," Kane answered, launching into a discussion about more editing things. I took the time to hear them all speak, get a sense of what kind of people they were.

Quinn was the consummate professional, BJ was quiet and meek, Kane was definitely in charge, Eve was there to make her husband look good, and Sharon listened but I could tell that she would challenge authority from the way she shook her head at stuff Kane was saying.

"Great, another cave to shoot in," Quinn said, adjusting his video camera.

"Don't worry, we'll fix it in post," Kane replied.

"I *am* post." Quinn laughed.

"Overall, respect the house," Kane said. I felt like maybe he was saying this for my benefit, since I'd told them the ghosts here didn't mess around. "Respect the spirits. If we want to get anything, we want them to invite us in. Got it?"

"Got it," they all mumbled then got around to getting ready. Eve blotted her husband's forehead of sweat then came around with more wipes to make Sharon camera-ready. Watching them work was fascinating, but I couldn't help but feel like this wouldn't last long.

Eve passed by me, stopped, retraced her steps, blotted my forehead with a smile and said, "You don't need this. You always look fabulous."

For the first time since arriving, I cracked a smile. At least there was Eve.

"Let's get an opening shot," Kane said, crossing his arms. All eyes were on Sharon. "Steady...roll tape in three..." He counted down on his fingers...two...one.

"Hello, I'm Sharon Roswell, and today we come to you from one of the deepest, darkest secrets of the Everglades—Villegas House. Built circa 1955 by local gladesmen, this two-story plantation home situated on a cypress island later became home to environmentalist Gregory H. Rutherford and his wife, Elena Villegas, after the original builder abandoned it due to unclear circumstances. Is Villegas House haunted? We'll soon find out."

She went on to explain how the couple rehabilitated endangered species injured from hunting then released them back into the wild. How Roscoe Nesbitt's sons, William and Richard, harassed the new residents on the property and how the family feud lasted a couple of years until 1967 when everything went horribly wrong and police found six dead bodies, the seventh death happening in a nearby hospital.

I wondered where she'd gotten her information. It seemed she had studied it previously and only asked me for my version to verify it.

"Locals say the house is so haunted, nobody gets past the front door. Well, we're going to change that today, aren't we?" Sharon asked dramatically. Suddenly, right in the middle of filming, a loud noise, like a bang of wood, crashed inside of the house. "Did you hear that?" Sharon's eyes scanned the area, the camera following her at every expression.

Kane and BJ exchanged looks, and Eve seemed happy that things were already starting to happen by the way she silently clapped her fingertips together.

"Let's go inside and take a look…"

Sharon walked up the disheveled steps of Villegas House and touched the front door, which was wide open, with her fingertips.

"Shit. I don't know, you guys...it feels oppressive in there." She looked at the camera and shook her head. I knew this was part acting to create suspense viewers would eat up, and that "shit" would get bleeped out.

What we'd all heard was more than likely pieces of wood falling, literally rotting away, as we stood here, and if anything happened to Sharon Roswell, it would be nobody's fault but ShadowBox Productions' own.

Still, I stared at the house, drawn to it, as the sounds around me fell away. Something seemed to call to me, made my stomach clench and my heart palpitate. Were those whispers, telling me to stay away, other voices asking who I was, who we all were? No, it couldn't have been. I shook it off. My nervous brain was messing with me.

Behind me was Linda, still sitting in her chair, holding a clipboard and a pencil, still doing her crossword puzzle, but she looked far from entertained. The woman shook her head. "We shouldn't go in there," she mumbled.

Her voice sounded deeper, not as melodious as before.

Kane shushed her with two fingers held up. He continued to watch, as I did, the two big monitors BJ had set up showing Sharon and Quinn walking into the condemned house.

"But I understand," Linda mumbled again. "All in the name of research."

I got a sense of dread hearing Linda, the one woman they should all be listening to, telling us that we shouldn't go in there.

"It's why we came," Kane told Linda then looked at me with wide eyes, silently communicating that sometimes, things got tense on the set.

I could see how a medium's impressions might

interfere with a smooth production. Eyes back on the house, I watched as Sharon slowly made her way inside, then within seconds, she and Quinn had disappeared into the gloom. My eyes shifted to the monitors, which changed to the grainy image I often saw on TV when they were filming in the dark. Suddenly, the screen turned black with only white lines breaking up the darkness.

"What's going on?" Kane asked BJ.

"We lost connection."

"Damn it. Keep rolling. Quinn, Sharon, you all right?" Kane asked.

A few moments later, the host and the cameraman reemerged from the house, shaking their heads. Sharon wiped sweat off her brow and gave Eve a look like that didn't go well, while Quinn walked all the way up to the tech station.

"Camera's dead," he said.

"What do you mean?" Kane asked. "Dead-dead, or?"

"Dead," Quinn replied. "It just turned off while we were walking through the first room. I tried turning it back on, and you know I charged the shit out of it before we started, so I don't know what the hell's happening."

"What's happening is the spirits don't want you inside."

Linda again.

We all looked at her, dark eyes gazing ahead at a spot on the ground in front of her, unfocused. Her hand holding the pencil skittered across the page, scratching out on the paper. Something about her looked…off.

"She's doing it again," Kane mumbled to his wife.

"They don't want you," Linda mumbled. She scribbled harshly now, ripping into the paper. Quinn took hold of a different camera and rushed over to stand behind her. I shifted my spot to see what she was writing as well. She held the pencil in a fist, child-like, trance-like, staring straight ahead, as though someone else were writing messages through her.

And there, in large chicken-scratch letters was the word—DIE.

EIGHT

"What is that supposed to mean?"

"Did she just write DIE?"

"Did you catch that? Did everyone see that?" Sharon spoke dramatically into the camera as it filmed Linda.

I'd seen enough episodes to know how this would end up in post-production. These were the snippets when the host, in a voiceover, said things like, *Suddenly, our medium, Linda Hutchinson, who'd been sitting peacefully at our camp, began channeling messages from beyond the grave...*

But Linda didn't seem to be acting to me. She continued to scratch the paper with her pencil point following the same grooves, over and over again—DIE, DIE, DIE—her eyes wide and full of a panicked emptiness.

Sharon reached out and placed her hand over the paper to get Linda to stop. "Linda? It's okay. Come out of it, dear. We're all here," she said then louder into the air, "You want us to die, spirits? Is that what this message means? Well, we're not here to do that. We're here to find out who you are and what happened here in 1967."

If they asked me, the spirits did not care to discuss why they were trapped here or what happened to them.

My tribe members had said it many times before—the restless souls at Villegas House were not eager to go into the light. They were eager for us to join them.

I shook my head and told myself that all was fine, that the poor woman obsessively scribbling the word DIE on the piece of paper was not in any way freaking me out whatsoever. I needed to get out of here a minute and clear my head space.

Walking toward the airboat, I briefly imagined taking off in it all by myself and leaving them behind. I could never do that, yet I couldn't shake the image. I shouldn't have come here. I shouldn't.

"Avila?" It was Eve calling to me.

I held a hand up while walking and stopped to catch my breath.

A moment passed, and she muttered, "She just needs space. It was too much for her."

Maybe it was. I'd never seen such a thing in all my life. Had that been real-life possession or acting for the camera's sake? Who would tell us to *die* like that?

Once at the riverbank, I stopped cold. Lined up near the airboat were three alligators—large, perched on the mangroves, black bumpy snouts with mouths open, hissing the moment they saw me. It wasn't unusual to see alligators in the Everglades—I saw them every day. What was strange was that they kept their distance. Alligators loved to climb up onto the land to bask in the sunshine when they were tired, but these gators seemed to want nothing to do with the house and remained resting half in the water, half on the cypress roots.

It made me think about how police were surprised to find the dead bodies here untouched by alligators after the massacre.

"I don't blame you," I told them. The hissing

stopped, but they continued to keep a wary eye on me. If they could get past their fear of Villegas House, they would be all over our camp. After a few minutes of clearing my head, I trudged back and informed Kane, "We need to move closer to the house. At least four feet above the water level."

"Why? What's wrong?"

"Gators. But don't tell the others. Trust me."

Last thing these people needed was to know that predatory reptiles surrounded the airboat a mere thirty yards from camp. They weren't hurting us and didn't seem like they would come nearer. Still, non-Florida people always freaked out about alligators, and we didn't need more alarm. After seeing Linda channel the word DIE from an unseen spirit, assuming it hadn't been theatrics, it was better that way.

By six o'clock, the crew had not yet re-started filming, and I was beginning to think we would stay the presumed "last resort" night over.

They'd spent the better part of the day trying to get the faulty camera working, only to discover their interior spare not turning on either. The last camera was for exterior shots, which they refused to take inside the house. I could feel Kane's frustration growing the more our daylight sank beneath the horizon.

Staying out of the way for most of it, I decided Linda looked like enough time had elapsed to approach her about what had happened. I pulled up a camp chair next to hers where she sat reading a book. "No pencils this time, huh?" I asked.

She gave me a sheepish look. "Sorry if that scared you."

"Hell, yeah, it scared me. I've never seen anyone do

that before. Was that you writing?"

"It was me, my hands, but no, that wasn't my message."

"Were you aware of what you were writing? It almost looked like you wanted to kill someone the way you were stabbing that pencil into the paper."

"I wasn't aware at that moment, no. It's like meditation when you're in an alpha state. Have you ever meditated?"

"Not in the yoga sense, but I do zone out on the boat sometimes. It's my sacred space."

"You see and hear what's going on behind a sheet of glass?" she asked.

"Yes." That was a good way to describe it. But I didn't want to talk about the way I sometimes tapped into the other side, because it scared the shit out of me. I switched focus. "Linda, who was telling you to write 'die?'" I asked, picking up a blade of sawgrass and running my thumb along its jagged edges.

"Something dark. I don't know *who* it is. It's in charge of this house, maybe of this whole island. We do many of these investigations where I warn them about an evil presence, but it's their job to proceed. Still, I can't help but wonder if one of these investigations won't be their last."

The lines around her eyes told of years' worth of witnessing odd things. Even though I didn't envy her job, I envied how many places she'd been and the world she'd seen. And if I zoned out and looked at her hard enough, I saw something else…

Disease…

I sat back in my folding chair and stared at her.

Where that word had come from, I didn't know. But there it was. I looked at Linda. Linda looked at me like she knew that I knew something about her. Until she mentioned it, though, I wouldn't. Still, it did make me wonder why she was here to begin with if, in fact, she was ill. Her dark, kind eyes reminded me of someone I couldn't place.

"That's why I've never come here before. I have too much respect for the other world."

"I do, too, Avila. But something about having me here makes them feel better. The messages which come to me corroborate their findings. They get hunch feelings that dark presences exist, and I verify them."

"Then, why bring you on at all?"

"Sometimes they have trouble communicating. Their Ovilus III will stop working, messages won't come through, they need somebody sensitive." She scoffs. "It's funny. Any one of them could do what I do. It takes years of meditation and practice. We all have psychic ability to varying degrees. Still, they prefer their techy things."

"It's easier," I said.

"And faster. But you…" The waning light had turned her eyes a shade of golden amber. "You could do what I do."

I shook my head. "Oh, no. I can't. I'm too chicken shit. I mean, I love *telling* ghost stories. I love ghost lore from afar. I could never be hands-on involved with them, day in, day out like you."

I said the same thing about giving airboat rides.

What can *I do day in, day out?*

At least Linda employed her talents by helping others, warning them, facing the unknown. When I reached her age, I hoped to be as useful to others, but the way my life was going, I didn't see that happening.

"You're young, Avila," Linda said, glancing at me. "I didn't develop my skills until much later in life. Middle age has a way of making you face things you never wanted to face. You're better off in the end, though."

She closed her eyes for a much-needed break, and I got up and walked toward the woods, hoping to ground myself again. Being in the camp made me feel claustrophobic. Normally, I'd love spending the day on a cypress island, checking out wildlife, searching for animal tracks, observing nature at its finest, but this particular island felt devoid of life. Oppressive. Something stagnant in the air sucked the vitality right out of it. It felt like it needed a good sage energy clearing.

As I felt the first drops of rain, the air cooled down significantly. The storms had come late today. Afternoon rain in the Everglades were an everyday occurrence in the summer. With so much heat, marsh water evaporated when the sun was at its hottest, then the clouds, unable to contain their fill, spilled every afternoon. Sometimes it fell in torrents, and tourists would ask if this was normal.

It was.

Except as the droplets began falling, I could tell this would be a hard torrential rain. I could hear Kane giving orders to put all equipment into the cases and bring them into the tents for the duration of the storm. Even with all the hubbub around me, I felt myself distancing from the rest of the team. I walked toward the edge of the property where the denser woods began.

Something was in there.

Someone was…

…calling me.

Most likely, it was in my mind, but I heard my name echoing from a distant place. When I paused to listen with closed eyes, I felt my whole body trembling—no, vibrating—gently. It could've been the earth underneath my feet, spiking energy through me, especially with the rain pounding, soaking my patchwork blouse, the elements coming together to amplify sensations. But the vibrations got stronger until I felt they were coming *from* me.

Avila.

I opened my eyes, stared ahead. The cypress trees with their long, thin trunks and bulbous roots reaching into the watery ground looked like people standing there, legs apart, facing off with me. Cognitively, I knew they were trees, just like I knew this was rain falling, but I couldn't help feel like they were alive. Of course they were alive, Avila, but alive, in the human sense, as though they were watching me, inviting me in.

Get away from those people. They are not like you.
They want to exploit the house, this land, but you respect it.
Come with us.

I didn't hear these words like I'd hear normal words. They coursed through my veins, whispered to me suggestively, like a flowing river or an electrical current.

People.

The trees looked like people, and the darker the sky got, the heavier the rain, the more insidious their shapes appeared. Hunched over... The more the gray clouds took over, creating a hazy neutral tone over the woods where it was difficult to tell what was what.

Avila...

Was that...

My brother?

I knew that voice. I'd know it anywhere. I'd heard it at least a hundred times a day when I was a kid. I'd even wished he'd stop calling me so often, as older sisters often did wish their pesky little brothers would go away. But at this moment, I felt myself wanting to hear him again.

"Billie?" My voice shook. Was it really him?

If it was, would the dark energy be with him? To this day, I still didn't know what I had seen lingering in the background the night he visited me in my sleep, but I always imagined that I'd see it again if Billie returned.

I waited.

It definitely sounded like him, but why would he, or his spirit, be in this place? Billie had died on the roadside of US-41, and I always thought ghosts lingered wherever they were known to have passed away. Maybe he was a figment of my imagination.

"Billie, is that you? I'm sorry for what happened…" I said, my voice cracking. "I'm sorry I let you sit in the front seat. I shouldn't have switched with you." It should've been me on the other side, not him.

The trees continued to be nothing but trees while channeling human energy at the same time. I knew I wasn't alone, had never been out here or anywhere. No matter where I went, someone was always watching. From the moment we'd arrived on this island, they'd been watching us from the woods.

They're out there—the dead.

It's not fair…

"What's not fair, Billie?" I narrowed my eyes so my vision could focus on one particular tree that seemed to move, take slow steps, until a little boy came around the bend, emerging from the shadows. A little boy I had loved so much, my heart ached every day just knowing I'd never see him alive again. He wore the same clothes as the day of the accident—blue jeans and the sewn traditional top my mother had made him.

You got to live.

I knew it.

My head dropped. The tears came.

"Yes, Billie. I got to live while you had to die. Damn

it. I'm so sorry for that..." It'd always lingered in my mind—the debilitating guilt that I'd survived the crash. Sometimes I wondered if I really got the better deal out of it, though. My life hadn't meant much so far, whereas he got to explore the cosmos, Heaven, wherever he was.

When I was finished feeling sorry for myself, I opened my eyes again, but this time, it wasn't Billie I saw coming around a cypress tree like a slithering wisp of fog. For a moment, I worried it was the dark energy that had accompanied him long ago.

Instead, a young woman stood in the middle of the woods staring at me, long reddish-brown hair hanging down either side of her face. She was beautiful with smooth pale skin, like a porcelain doll made from bone china. My heart raced, not only because this spirit stood there studying me, but because I knew her.

NINE

I shouldn't have recognized her.

I'd never seen her before, and yet I felt like I'd known her every day of my life. Her hair was long, flowing. Eyes bright and understanding. I knew the way she moved—fluidly, like underwater—the way her dress poured out behind her. She stepped out of the trees toward me, and once she hit the rain, was gone.

She looked like a much younger Linda. Could I have been seeing a projection?

Disease…

Suddenly, I feared it was her. Was Linda okay, or was I seeing a form of her ghost?

I bolted back to camp, tripping over logs, scampering through the cypress trees. She hadn't been looking too well all day, and I had an impression of her being sick. The moment I arrived back at camp, Sharon asked where Linda was. I didn't want to mention just having seen her in the woods as a young woman, so I kept my mouth shut and helped look for her.

"She was here half an hour ago," Sharon said.

"We have to find her," I said urgently.

Sharon gave me a cursory look. "Why do you say it like that? Is she okay?" She broke into a faster hustle, searching in each tent and around the house. "She wouldn't have gone inside the house, would she?"

Kane stepped up to us. "You guys looking for Linda? I thought she was with you."

"I thought she was with you," Sharon said.

"Crap." Kane, Sharon, and I split into different directions, and I found myself hovering near the cypress trees again. I felt drawn to them, though my nerves were shot knowing that one of us would probably find the old woman dead at any moment.

Out of the corner of my eye, I saw a flash of white and saw a shirt, an arm, a leg scuttling on the ground, like a roach on its back trying to get up from a pile of dry brush.

"Linda!" I ran to her. She was down but not dead. As relieved as I was, seeing her struggling to get up also left me confused. Who, then, who had I seen out in the trees? "Are you okay? Guys, she's here!" I called out.

Sharon and Kane ran over while I helped Linda to a sitting position. She'd had the wind knocked out of her. "Something led me..." Linda struggled to breathe. "Something called me out here."

"Something called me, too," I said. I gave her both my hands, as Kane stood behind her, placing his hands on her middle back. Sharon and I hoisted the woman to her feet. "A young lady. She told me her name, but now I can't remember it."

"Did you fall? What happened?" I asked once she was on her feet.

"I don't know. I...lost consciousness."

"Let's get her to the tent and aim a fan on her," Kane told us. "We'll plug the one that's on the tech onto her directly, so she can get some fresh air. It's stifling out here."

We carried Linda to the tents and sat her down, positioning one of the two small portable fans directly on her, so she could catch her breath. Bringing her a bottle of cold water from the cooler, I twisted it open and handed it to her. It only took a minute for her to regain her color.

"You scared me," I told her. I really didn't know what we would've done had Linda passed away out here, and I was at even more at a loss to explain the ghost woman in the forest if it hadn't been her. I might have witnessed the spirit of either of the women who'd been murdered here in 1967, but I was pretty sure, having seen photos of Elena Villegas on the internet, that she'd been olive-skinned and dark-haired.

"I'm sorry," Linda said, eyes closed, water bottle in hand. "I can feel it, though."

"Feel what?" I asked.

I knew her answer before she even said it. I knew because some kind of shift had been happening to me from the moment I arrived here, one that opened me up to currents of information to which I shouldn't have been privy.

"My time," she replied. "It's coming."

In the evening, after an unappetizing dinner of canned pork and beans heated on a portable burner, Kane announced we'd be spending the night. They'd gotten very little done during the shoot today thanks to the faulty equipment but he hoped that tomorrow would be better. If they continued to have issues, they'd cut the expedition short and call it a loss. If anyone wasn't feeling up to snuff, Kane also said, now was the time to say it so we could return to the village and part ways.

I asked Linda if she was okay enough to stay. "You

sure?"

"I haven't felt well in years, dear, but I'm not going to leave. They have work to do in that house," Linda said, going back to her crossword puzzles. "They don't make their investment back, they don't get paid. Kids don't eat."

"Kids?"

"Kane and Eve. Got a boy back home, a girl just started college."

"Ah."

It must've been difficult for her to come along on these investigations, be the one person who connected the most with psychic energy, but remain neutral on the decision-making part of the process. Linda Hutchinson was their puppet. And their trooper.

Kane looked at me inquisitively since I was talking to Linda, as if asking for a report on how she felt. I gave him a thumb's up to express that Linda seemed fine. "Alright then, hope you all get some sleep. Anybody need anything from the food tent before I close it?"

"I do." I scrambled over to the big plastic tub containing the dry packaged foods and cans and grabbed a granola bar. The pork and beans hadn't done it for me. As I was heading out of the tent, Kane held onto my arm.

"Did she seem okay to you?" he asked, worry lines on his forehead.

"I think she's a little worn down, but she seems okay now."

"You sure?"

"I think so. She's in good spirits, doing her crosswords."

Kane laughed a shallow laugh in his chest. "Yeah, she loves those. Alright. Since you're sleeping in the same tent as her, keep an eye on her, will you? Linda's been with us too long, and I'd hate for her to feel sick and not tell us. She's done it before. Kind of a martyr, if you know what I mean."

"Sure. I get it." And with that, I headed to bed, knowing I wouldn't get a wink of sleep. Hoping to God that nothing would visit me in my dreams. I unrolled the sleeping bag the crew had brought for me and lay on top. It was too hot to get inside a flannel-lined cocoon, so I lay over it staring up at the apex of the tent ceiling.

"I'm sorry if I scared you out there," Linda said from her chair by the open flap of the tent. "I'm afraid this place is affecting me more than any other I've been in recent years. I used to be affected quite a bit when I first started coming along on investigations, but this one…this one is different."

"Different how?" I rolled up the top side of the sleeping bag to form a soft pillow and readjusted myself until I was somewhat comfortable.

"The entities here are older than most houses. More primitive and powerful. I told them in Atlanta that coming here wouldn't be a good idea."

"They said it was a unique location."

"Is that what they said?" Linda harrumphed, closed her crossword puzzle book, and slowly stood. She moaned in the typical way older folks did about their aches and pains and joints upon standing. "Goodnight, everybody." She waved to the tech crew that was still doing some work out by the lantern.

Everyone bid her goodnight, then she lowered her head and came into the tent. Eve had been nice enough to double up sleeping bags for Linda, and I would've given her my own for a third if I didn't need it myself.

"You know," she said, out of breath, lowering to a seated position on the ground. "I do these for another reason too."

"What's that?" I asked.

"When I was younger, I didn't fully accept my gifts. I wanted them gone." She spoke as she got her things ready for bed. "There were so many people who would've given an arm and a leg for my abilities, but here I had them and wanted nothing to do with them."

Linda pulled a small bottle out of her bag, uncapped it and placed a tiny pill onto her tongue before taking a swig of water from her bottle.

"As I got older, I realized this was why I was here. I'd been given this gift for a reason, and that was to help people. You shouldn't be afraid of your gifts either, Avila."

Looking at Linda, I saw the honesty in her face, the exhaustion in her eyes. She'd lived a good—what—sixty or seventy years? I couldn't tell, but it had been long enough to accrue the kind of wisdom I should definitely listen to. I just wasn't sure "gift" was the right word.

"But I *am* afraid of them," I said.

Linda rested her head on a small pillow. "That will either change with time or with circumstance," she said, turning off her flashlight. "Whichever comes first. I do think this will be my last, though."

"Why do you say that?"

"Look at this old lady getting into a sleeping bag, Avila. But I came to help someone find closure, so I want to make sure she gets it."

Sometime in the night, I awoke to a revelation.

Panting, catching my breath, I'd been dreaming about Sharon and why she'd asked me all those questions the day before. It wasn't for the show. She wanted to know for herself. She had a personal connection to Villegas

House, and Linda had told her that I would take her here. That was why Kane and Eve had sought me out. She said a Miccosukee woman would know about the house, and when they'd done their research, they'd found—me.

Why did Sharon want to find *this* house, of all houses? It couldn't have meant anything to her. Around me, the silence felt unsettling. A quick look at my phone told me it was 3 AM. I'd been asleep several hours.

Linda had told me I shouldn't be afraid of my gifts, and that was all I could dream about for half the night. No matter what images my brain had conjured up in the night, I could hear Linda's voice in the perimeter telling me it was useless to be afraid. The spirits could be menacing, but they couldn't hurt me—not physically anyway.

I wasn't so sure.

I'd seen episodes of their show where Sharon would get scratched, or finger marks would press against someone's throat. Right now, the crickets had quieted, and that, in and of itself, scared me. Did something walk outside the tent? The more I drifted in and out of sleep, the more I felt it was something physical, of this earth.

Feet scuttling, hands grasping.

Whispering.

I sat up on my sleeping bag and listened. I might have been dreaming. My mind may have been playing tricks on me, but sure enough, I heard hushed voices and twitching sounds. The voices were not familiar, or even human, and then I heard the crunch of plastic and metal being hashed around. Was someone messing with the equipment?

I wouldn't be able to sleep again until I knew.

These wild areas of Big Cypress could be dangerous if you weren't vigilant. I didn't want to find out too late that a wild hog or kowi—panther—had been on the prowl near my guests. Shuffling to my feet, I crawled to the tent flap, unzipped it open, and went outside. Just in case, I grabbed my phone, turned on the video, and got it ready.

TEN

Surrounded by tents, camp chairs, coolers, and our makeshift kitchen, I stood in the darkness and listened. Not a single movement. Not a shift of branch or leaf coming from the woods. In the stillness, I closed my eyes, detecting the very normal, very human sounds of loud breathing and snoring.

From the trees came a silence that permeated my soul.

Even nature wasn't that quiet.

The heroic part of my brain wanted to explore, assure the security of the crew's safety as they slept, make sure no panthers were prowling, but the other part of me, the part that had been imbued with fear of the unknown since a young age felt paralyzed.

Evil was out there, like the things I'd seen long ago.

I felt them.

What if ghosts watched us from the perimeter? What if they'd been waiting for us to fall asleep so they could invade our dreams, take our souls? Then I'd capture them on video, hand the footage over to the crew, and get the hell out of here. Scanning the camp, a million scenarios ran through my mind, not a single one of them practical or reasonable.

Avila.

No. No, I'd seen this movie before, the one where the unsuspecting scream queen followed the sound of her name being called, leading to inevitable danger. There was no way I'd follow. No way, except the voice sounded like Billie's, or the way my brain attempted to piece together the memory of Billie. Why would my little brother be here in the middle of the Everglades? Maybe he was always with me, and only now did I notice.

"Billie?" I watched the darkness through the staticky phone screen.

The glades' heat and humidity did nothing to quench the chills on my skin.

"Billie?" I called again.

Whispers carried through the humid air.

My skin pricked with goose bumps.

I floated through the camp in an out-of-body experience, except I *was* walking. I felt the peat moss and cool moist dirt on the ground beneath my feet, the vibrations of the ground rising through my legs, the phone trembling in my hand. All reminded me I was alive. Mortal. Made of flesh, unlike whatever stalked the swamp. In fact, I'd never been more alert in my life, more tuned-in to the world around me, but which world— which dimension—did I walk?

Villegas House—the wood, the sagging roof, the shingles—existed on one plane.

Its heart and soul existed in another.

And it watched.

I stood facing the house. If I squinted just enough, the windows looked like manic eyes carved from a jack-o-lantern and the eaves looked like disheveled eyebrows, and that front door… I shook my head. This was nuts. There was no way the house was alive or real or looked like a face, or looked like it was grinning, or calling me, or any such imaginings. It was 3 AM, damn it, and I was under the influence of sleep with the sharpness of a woken mind.

Avila…

"No." I shook my head, tried to squeeze the voice from my head. "No, Billie. You're not here. You're in my memory. This house is just trying to get me to come in."

Above me, a pair of shutters slammed together and wavered back and forth in the breeze. I ripped my gaze away from the slumping structure and looked at my feet to make sure I wasn't dreaming. Bare, dirty feet firmly rooted in the grass. The house wanted me to stare it down, challenge it, step inside, but there was no way I would.

I was about to turn off my video when to my right, I heard the whispers again, only this time they didn't sound like people discussing in hushed tones. They didn't sound human or ethereal either. Taking steps toward the camp's supplies tent, I paused to listen. Skitterings, if that was a word. Scuttling and discussion and scheming. The tent shook gently, stopped, then shook again. Half my brain knew it was critters, more than likely, but the other half…

Come into the house, Avila.

We need you.

"No," I told the voice. There was nothing special about me. I was an ordinary woman with an ordinary life. No way did ghosts know my name or need me. This was my brain, my sick, deluded brain playing tricks on me. "Go away."

I could do this.

Coming around the side of the tent, I spotted it—the perfect cut-out window in the nylon siding and immediately knew what was going on. I crept up slowly, because what if it wasn't? What if something besides critters were inside that tent?

Avila, you're psyching yourself out.

I had seen this same scenario before. Anyone who lived in a natural habitat had. Swallowing my dread, I pushed aside my nerves and let the rational side of my mind take the reins. I pulled back the loose piece of nylon wavering in the minimal breeze, and peeked inside.

Several sets of beady little black eyes looked back at me, frozen with guilt.

A tsunami of relief washed over me so hard, my knees buckled. Raccoons I could deal with. Raccoons were of this world. Raccoons were harmless.

"Shoo! Get out of here," I ordered the creatures. Little trash pandas had ripped a perfect incision into our supplies tent, opened the Rubbermaid containers with their nimble hands, and were chowing down on granola bars and raw hot dogs.

The raccoons shrieked then scattered. They jumped out of the tent and left a mess in their wake. They bolted into the woods, bouncing and criss-crossing each other in panic while I stood there gripping my freaked-out heart. "Shit."

In the night and darkness, they'd sounded like bandits. I wasn't the only one awake now, as I tuned into real human voices crossing the camp. Familiar figures emerged from the dark and joined me at the scene of the crime.

"What happened?" Quinn, fully dressed, and Kane, in only shorts and no shirt, crawled up to me. I averted my eyes from Eve's shirtless husband and looked at Quinn instead. In his hand, he held a shotgun aimed at the ground.

Seriously?

"Raccoons got into our food," I said, gazing at Quinn's weapon. What was he doing with that thing? Nobody told me there'd be a gun at this camp. Shouldn't there have been full disclosure of that at our initial meeting?

"Wasn't it closed up?" Kane whispered.

"Doesn't matter," I said. "Knowing how to get to food is their specialty."

Kane peeked past me, craning his neck to view the carnage. All inside the tent floor were open wrappers, container lids, and punctured sports drink bottles. A soupy, nasty mess. Quinn peeked in as well, shaking his head. "Little shits."

Yes, they were, but raccoons weren't the problem. Besides a perfect stranger toting a weapon around me, about ten feet away lying motionless on the ground was a small four-legged plump furry body. "Look there."

Kane stepped closer to the corpse already abuzz with angry flies. One raccoon hadn't fared as well as the others. It'd been ripped open, its black and brown body torn to shreds, entrails everywhere, a pudding cup still in its dexterous little hands. "What the hell?" Kane covered his mouth.

Quinn got in close to examine the raccoon then began checking for tracks. "What could've done this? Panther?" He aimed the gun into the woods, a cowboy ready for anything.

Kane must've seen the worry on my face, because he touched Quinn's arm and made him lower it with a quiet shake of his head. "Not now."

"Then when?" Quinn retorted.

I looked past everyone at the woods. "A panther wouldn't have mangled it. Panthers hunt and eat, not murder for sport." The animal hadn't been eaten. Instead, something had torn it apart without taking any of its meat.

"Then, what did this?" Kane asked.

"I don't know." We could crawl back into our tents, but the thin nylon walls would provide us with zero protection. "Maybe we should leave the island."

He looked at me, hands on his hips, lips pressed together. What was going on in that man's mind? Something to do with ratings, viewership and lost investment, most likely.

"Let's get this cleaned up," Kane said, looking around. "Quinn, help me put the animal in a garbage bag. We'll double-bag it and hope the smell doesn't attract anything else."

Kane gave me a knowing look. He knew about the nearby gators, because I'd mentioned them, but this wasn't made by a predator.

"Guys," I said. "Something mangled that raccoon, something that didn't even want to eat it. I don't know any animal that would do this, and I've lived in this area my whole life."

The men listened but ignored me for the most part. It was clear they had no plans on leaving any time soon, certainly not in the middle of the night, and not until they'd captured something that could be minimally produced into an episode.

Maybe I was freaking out for no reason. A wild hog could have ripped apart the raccoon, one that had been thwarted when I came to investigate. Maybe I was wrong and panthers were hunting tonight. I had to calm down.

"Should we shoot this?" Quinn hoisted the shotgun over his shoulder.

It took me a moment to realize he meant shooting footage.

"Yeah, go ahead," Kane said. "Get the camera. A few good angles and pics for studying later. I don't know how to approach all this, I'll tell you that much."

"It's been more about the living than the dead," Quinn added.

In hushed tones, they talked about the show and how to package the shots they'd taken so far. Here I was, worried about whatever was in the house that wanted to harm us, and these guys' minds were still on the show.

I realized my own video had been running, but I'd had it aimed at the floor for the last few minutes. Turning it off, I put the phone back in my pocket and slowly backed away from the men.

The house looked at me again. I stared back at the monster.

I won't go inside, I told it.

Looming in the darkness, its mouth—the front door—yawned wide open.

We all looked at it.

What did it want with me? Why did it taunt me? I might have been losing my mind. A raccoon had been torn to shreds a few feet from its front porch for no apparent reason, had not been carried off by its predator—I had a right to panic. Just in front of it were two men, obsessed over documenting the event, and inside my tent was an old woman who had warned us that something wanted us to die.

I didn't want to stay. I didn't want to enter the tent either.

What if Linda was wide awake, staring at the doorway with those vacant eyes, channeling DIE DIE DIE again? Empty of soul and filled with another's energy. In the distance, I heard the thrashing of water and knew that the alligators were arguing, fighting over what morsels of food they had found. Though they continued to stay away, I knew gators were curious creatures and would eventually want to see what we were up to.

We had to leave in the morning. I'd do whatever I could to convince them. I knew chances were slim, because I had little evidence of anything wrong, except for the raccoon and my *feelings*, but I couldn't explain my fear.

My people had been right. Had been for years. Villegas House was not to be messed with. As though the island wanted to prove my point for me, a cool breeze blew through, rattling the tents, winds of sweet, heavy rain. Overhead, vast dark clouds rumbled. Big Cypress was about to catch a summer storm, and the crew of *Haunted Southland* would finally get a taste of a real thunderstorm. The choices were to stick to our tents, airboat back to the village under a deluge to threaten all technical equipment, or seek shelter inside Villegas House itself.

I would've taken any of those options, except the last.

ELEVEN

The sky opened, as shards of rain pelted us like bullets. Everglades thunderstorms were no joke, and this crew was about to learn the hard way that their tents were no match. Camp broke into a panic, as everyone scattered to collect things.

Sharon shot out of her tent in unbuttoned shorts and tank top.

Linda and BJ shuffled out of their tents, as we all rushed to gather bags, equipment, pillows, blankets, anything we could carry. "You take this! I'll take that bag!" Linda shouted.

Detached, I watched the crew scamper.

"Bring it all into the house!" Kane shouted through the deluge.

While I'd been caught in many *Kahayatle* thunderstorms during airboat tours, this one was special. I hadn't seen it moving in. I was usually adept at telling when it was about to pour, but the raccoon death had distracted me. The ghosts in the woods had distracted me. I wasn't myself, and that alone put me at unease.

Overhead, the sky boomed, raindrops splashed my sweaty skin and soaked my hair. A mixture of acrid and sweet scents rose from the earth, as rain hit peat moss, activating bacteria, living things from under the earth, even the stench of the dead raccoon through the garbage bag. Everything sprung to life. All I could do was stand there and watch. I loved the panic, felt like I'd seen this scene before in another lifetime long ago.

"Avila!" Linda shouted through the curtain of rain. "Avila, come on!"

Rooted to the spot. Like watching a dream unfold in my head through a different dimension than my own. I heard my name being called, but I couldn't respond nor spring into action.

Like déja-vu.

One by one, the crew disappeared into Villegas House.

I wouldn't join them.

Seeking shelter was the last thing on my mind, especially there. The storm infused me with an energy I couldn't place. Closing my eyes, I heard them—the voices I'd heard earlier. Voices plotting in hushed tones. It frustrated me to know so many things, but not who was talking. The unmistakable sound of an airboat grew in the distance then whizzed by. I couldn't believe that anyone would be out here boating at this time of night.

"Someone is here," I said to no one.

I stared straight through the cypress trees to the riverbank.

My God, I felt like I was going crazy, but yes, that had definitely been the sound of an airboat. Were gladesmen out for a nightly hunt? Heading toward the shore where we'd left our airboat tethered, I heard the shouts of the crew behind me trying to coax me to come back. I picked up speed through the needles of rain headed for the riverbank. Several times now I'd been drawn to an area for no apparent reason.

When spongy land slowly gave way to water and my feet became soaked, I spotted our boat tied to a tangle of mangrove roots and squinted to make sure the sound wasn't our own boat being stolen. I was sure I would hear the motor again, but there were no ripples or wake in the river, or any sign that anyone had been here. Less than twenty-four hours later, and already I was hearing things.

I wanted to be near the investigation—it was why I'd come—but I hadn't asked for this.

For a sixth sense, a third eye, psychic vision, whatever you wanted to call it, but maybe this was what my mother meant by inviting it in. *En maheem, Avila,* I could hear her now. *You asked for it.* Opening myself up was a bad thing. Fine. But how could I make it stop now that I was here?

Take the boat, a voice said.

I could do that easily, but no—God—I wouldn't. There was no way I could leave these people here stranded on this island to their own devices with a day's worth of food and no means of getting back. They'd die, not the kind of thing I needed on my conscience.

Without my knowledge of these lands, these people would perish.

"Avila!" The distant shouts snapped me out of my trance.

I was soaked from head to toe through my clothes. It felt damn good. Like awaking from a long cyclical dream out of which I could not escape, a hamster wheel of the neverendingness that was my life. The sounds of airboats dissipated like an echo in a canyon but something new replaced it. There, in the pouring rain surrounded by darkness, the humid woods, and a whole island abuzz with invisible energy came laughter.

My skin erupted into goose bumps. Chills ran through me.

Men's laughter.

They spoke to each other, the types of things men said when they were in on a joke and you were their female target. The types of things white gladesmen said when you walked into the Winn-Dixie on the edge of town wearing your patchwork skirt down to the floor instead of the shorts and T-shirts their little blond barefoot children wore.

Hey, dirty girl, your mama make you that? Come here.

I shook my head. The rain created a curtain of white noise all around. I shouldn't have been able to hear the men. I closed my eyes, not wanting to see them. I could run to the house where everybody was hiding from the rainstorm and calling for me, the house I wasn't supposed to visit, but now it was too late. I could stay out here with the trees that sheltered ghosts of the past wishing to taunt me.

I can give you some real clothes. They're in my van…

I didn't have to open my eyes to see them. They lived forever in my mind, as fresh as the day I'd run into them while my mother was cashing a check at the grocery store customer service. Most people were nice, but every now and then, *they* came out of the woodwork—hateful sons of bitches with no respect for other cultures, as if their nicotine-stained teeth and stringy hair hidden underneath Florida Marlins baseball caps were the finest examples of their kind.

Come on, come to my van. I put in a mattress just yesterday. It'll be fun…

"Go away," I gritted my teeth at them. "Go the hell away."

I hated the fathers. And the children, too, even though they didn't taunt me. I hated them because one day they would. The hate would be passed on like disease.

Why did they have to be rude? I'd never felt hatred for anyone until that day. I'd done a pretty good job of putting the memories away. You had to, or else you couldn't function. There was no use going around worried what people from other cultures thought of you.

"Leave me alone. Can't you ever leave me alone?" I muttered.

"Who are you talking to, love?" I felt cold hands gripping my arm and turned to see Linda standing next to me getting soaked. "Come on inside, Avila. Don't listen to them."

She understood.

For that, I was grateful. Anyone else would've told me I was crazy for talking to thin air, whether from my own mind or another realm. "Yes...okay..." I mumbled, letting Linda lead me away back through the trees toward the clearing where the camp had been but now was mostly empty except for a few plastic bags and Rubbermaid containers.

Still, I looked back twice to make sure the men and their children were gone.

The house gaped at me out of the darkness, and every cell of my soul fought going towards it. I stopped short of the crumbling structure about ten feet, while Kane and others stood at the door beckoning me to come inside. They were alive and drier than I was, but at what expense?

I had to put aside my kid fears and just walk in already, tell myself it was like any other house, and maybe it would become true. If we lied to ourselves enough, eventually we'd make our own reality.

"Come on, Avila, honey. It's okay." Linda tugged at my arm. I felt bad that her pretty red hair was now a plastered mop of dark auburn punctuated by light gray roots on top of her head. Her age showed through.

I nodded, staring up at the house.

The rain imbued the energies, didn't it?

A murder had taken place here. All for what? Over a house? For a spot of land which amounted to an invisible speck on a map? What was it with people fighting for land so damn much? Land didn't belong to us anyway. We borrowed it, along with time, rented it from Mother Earth.

"God, why is this so hard?" I heard myself say.

"I know, honey. But come on. It may not want us here, but it's not going to hurt us." She said that just to get me inside and out of the rain, but I knew it wasn't true. The thing that came for me in the dark when I was little…that thing wanted to hurt me. I'd spent my life hiding from it.

"Oh, for hell's sake, just leave her out there if she doesn't want to come in."

The voice belonged to Sharon speaking just out of range near the open doorway. She must've thought I couldn't hear her, though I watched the accompanying hand flail to her words like I was a used rag to be forgotten about.

"Catching a cold for trying to help that woman is the last thing Linda needs. Come on, Linda!" Sharon bellowed.

Linda tugged on my arm, and finally, after a series of three quick bolts of nearby lightning in a row, I moved. Not because of the lightning, but because I didn't want to get the poor woman in trouble, make her look like a fool for helping me out.

"There you go, honey. Come on…" She ushered me up the porch steps and through the front door into the darkest house I'd ever been in my life.

Inside were pine wood walls rotting away underneath a sagging ceiling that leaked with rain in multiple spots. The inside space felt warm, humid, and body-scented from the sweating pores of five individuals. In the middle was a staircase leading up into even darker recesses. To my right was a living room mostly empty except for a wooden cupboard inside which sat cracked old porcelain plates.

A wooden spindled chair sat lonely in the corner. To my other side was another empty room except for another two chairs that matched the one in what I suspected was a dining room. Everyone was scattered across both rooms, running their hands through their hair or fanning themselves with random objects—baseball hats, stapled papers from their belongings, or expired airline tickets. Rain leaked through the ceiling in the corners.

"We shouldn't be here," I said.

Everyone looked at me like I was an idiot. Being inside was the very reason they'd come, the whole purpose for the trip.

"We won't be here for long, Avila," Kane said. He knew I was afraid of this house. I'd only told him a hundred times the day I met him.

BJ walked up to me and handed me a mostly wet green towel with a few dry spots on it. "Here, for whatever that's worth," he said. It occurred to me that I hadn't heard the tone of his voice before this.

"Thanks." I took the towel and handed it to Linda, who'd begun coughing, instead so she could dry herself off. I couldn't shake the feeling of dread inside me, but I told myself it would be over soon.

"Alright." Kane turned on a flashlight-lantern combo and stood it upright in the middle of the floor before standing and addressing everyone with a big exhale. "Listen up, people. Things are not going well, obviously, and time is money. Looking at the radar is tough because cell service is spotty at best. I don't think this storm will last long—"

"It won't," Quinn interrupted. "Everglades storms are flashes in the pan then they're over."

I loved how Quinn had suddenly become the Everglades expert.

"Well, this don't look like it's going to be over anytime soon," Sharon mumbled under her breath. "In fact, it's getting worse and all our equipment's gonna go to shit."

"Our equipment is fine. We came prepared. Watertight cases, plenty of plastic lining. Let's not jump to conclusions," Kane said to placate the hostess who had long ago gotten on my nerves.

For her lack of manners? For her brusqueness, I wasn't sure. All I knew was that she kept giving me dirty looks not unlike the ones I'd been reminded of outside with those old memories.

"We knew this could happen before we came, remember? We talked about the rainstorms and how they could put a damper on things, no pun intended."

Eve, wanting everyone to agree with her husband, as always, sat on the floor looking up at him, nodding, checking the crew's faces for understanding. "We did. We talked about it." When her line of view caught mine, she smiled.

I looked away, not used to people being as nice. When I first met her, I thought Eve's likeability was fake, but now I realized she was real. And she was some kids' mom, too, which made me like her even more.

"Right. So, my suggestion is we wait here in the house

for the rain to stop. Once it does, we film all we can. Alright, Sharon?"

"Assuming the damn cameras work," Sharon said.

"Obviously," Kane replied. "Catch whatever we can on tape, get the hell out of here. If it's a loss, it's a loss. This was risky from the beginning, best laid plans, and all that. Now—"

"So, you're saying we came out all this way for nothing?" Sharon crossed her arms. "Because I don't think I'm ready to go."

Nobody said anything. It seemed that nobody would dare. Only Kane, because he was in charge. Or was Sharon in charge?

"It happens, hon," Kane told her, flipping his palms up.

"Don't 'hon' me, Kane."

"Okay, what do you want me to do?" Kane bit back.

Sharon scoffed. "Don't you think we should stop at nothing to get what we want, especially since we've already been through so much? I mean, shit. First, the flights were delayed, then we had to pay triple for the damn airboat because nobody was a licensed operator when we rented it. Then Linda here tells us we're going to DIE, then a stupid raccoon up and flips over. Then, the rainstorm from Hell nearly ruins all our equipment. I mean, we're here, damn it, let's just do this."

From across the room, Quinn nodded. He of the gun agreed they should stop at nothing. That didn't make me feel any better. Everyone else seemed to have mixed thoughts, from the way they avoided Sharon's gazes.

"Like I said, we're going to give it a go," Kane said as calmly as a man in his position could. "Once it stops raining. But like I said, some gigs are a loss, Sharon. You need to accept that."

"I don't need to accept shit, Kane. I came here to find the truth."

The truth?

I looked at Linda, but she played with a ragged thread hanging from the hem of her shirt. Was it me, or was everyone starting to get on each other's nerves now that we were inside the house? What was this about the truth? Some cases were a lost cause and Villegas House was one of them.

Kane sucked in a breath, looked at me, then back at her, as though this was not one conversation I was privy to. "I know this episode was your idea, Sharon, but you're asking me to bypass circumstances. We'll do what we can, but some houses don't want to speak with us, and I'm not going to stick around while wild animals get killed and the elements bear down on us just so you can find your answers."

I agreed wholeheartedly with Kane, though I wanted to know what answers it was that Sharon wanted. "Why the interest in this house?" I asked out of the blue.

Again, all eyes fell on me.

"I mean, most people have never even heard of it, but you talk like it's meaningful to you. Why?"

"Doesn't matter, Cypress. Just let it be."

"Tell me."

"I told you, let it be!" Blue eyes narrowed and warned me.

I looked at Linda who widened hers at me, as if urging me to do just that—let it go. Did Sharon have a connection to this house? If she did, I wanted to know about it. Hell, I deserved to know about it, considering my grandfather had been killed here. "What do you know about Villegas House?" I asked again.

Sharon whipped her head around at me. "Alright, you

know what? The problem isn't what I know, it's what I *don't* know. So, since it seems we're going to be losing our time and money here, Kane darling, why don't we hurry things up then and do what we always do when we're pressed for time and the spirits won't cooperate?"

"No," Eve said, shaking her head. "Absolutely not."

"Why not?" Sharon asked her. "You know it's the easiest way when the ghosts don't want to speak. Let's do this already."

"Do what? What is she talking about?" I leaned toward Linda.

"A séance." She closed her eyes and inhaled deeply. "She wants me to conduct a séance."

TWELVE

In all the episodes I'd watched, I hadn't seen them do a single séance, which was perfectly fine with me. The idea of having one always freaked the heck out of me. A bunch of people sitting around a table, holding hands, inviting the spirits to speak and possibly take over your body? No, thank you.

Not even would I participate in a séance to talk to my own brother.

What was dead was dead.

Let the spirits rest.

But the only thought skating through my mind at the moment was Uncle Bob and my mom at dinner two weeks ago telling me that, by telling ghost stories on my airboat, I'd be inviting in dark spirits. I didn't believe it at the time, didn't buy the connection they were trying to make, and yet here I was two weeks later, sitting crossed legged on the floor of Villegas House listening to Sharon Roswell suggest they hold a séance.

Why was I scared by the thought of one if I hadn't believed my mother?

The crew looked at Linda and waited for her input. Kane, Eve, Quinn, and BJ all seemed to be in favor of holding the séance if it meant possibly getting out of here faster, and Sharon was, of course, waiting on pins and needles. I thought for sure Linda would object. After all, she knew all about the negative energy associated with this house, so imagine my surprise when she shrugged and shook her head in defeat.

"This is the last time I'll do this, people."

"Linda, you don't have to do this," I whispered.

She ignored me. "I already told you the spirits don't want you or anybody in this house. It upsets them, shows them what they can no longer have—a life. But let's do this and get this over with. Maybe we can be done with it and leave by morning."

"Sounds like a plan." Kane clapped in that way he loved to do to get himself motivated.

I couldn't believe this.

It was almost five in the morning, we hadn't slept, and now we were about to invite the spirits to speak through a fragile woman. I wouldn't participate. I couldn't. When judgment day came for me and my camp asked if I had led this group of non-Indians to our most reviled, feared location, I would admit to taking them here and endure their disappointment, but I could not participate in these rituals.

I would sit nearby and observe from a safe distance, if there were such a thing.

Linda held out her hand to me, so I would help her up. I guided her to the side of the house that seemed driest, all the while I couldn't believe this was happening. Having a séance, a communication circle of the dead, in a murder house during a thunderstorm. Good God.

Linda sensed my trepidation. "The faster we do this, the faster we go home, right?" She patted my hand. "I'm so sorry we brought you into this, Avila."

"It's fine," I said though it wasn't. Why did I always

insist things were fine when they weren't? Evil was going to come pouring into this house faster than a waterfall of shit.

Kane gave orders to the crew who quickly set up their cameras and voice recorders and other tech stuff. I heard BJ telling Kane that the one camera which had malfunctioned earlier was still acting wonky though better than before. "Lock off the cam," Kane told him. "We'll need to open the aperture wide and boost two-stops. Drop some cans against the wall with some low red splash."

Quinn pulled a plastic film out of a bag, unfolded, and proceeded to place it on top of the camera, which he set up on a tripod. About ten minutes later, they were ready for their circle of death, and I wanted to scream, *This is not a good idea! Maybe in a peaceful home with a mischievous spirit whose name you wanted to know, but not here. Not at Villegas House.*

What if we called the murderer through?

I had zero say. I sat as far back from the circle as I could blending into the gray pall of the house. I didn't even so much as want my skin touching the walls if I could help it, so I lingered on the fringe. Clutching my gator tooth necklace, head atop my knees, I watched in silence. Maybe Linda was right and this was best. It would satisfy the crew's curiosity, give Sharon whatever the heck she was looking for, and be easy to produce into an episode. They could take footage of the séance and edit it into an easy, hour-long show later on without having to stay another full day.

We could leave by morning.

Linda rummaged through the bag Eve had handed her and began taking out what appeared to be a sage smudge wand, an abalone shell, little figurines of various saints, a white pillar candle, and a lighter. Once she lit the candle and gave Kane a nod, he turned off his flashlight and everyone fell into a circle with Linda. Taking the smudge wand and dipping it into the flame, Linda blew out the end and the wand smoked beautifully. Droplets of rain played at the edges of the candle.

"Smoke of air, fire of earth, cleanse and bless this home and hearth…" She chanted off a simple prayer that had me feeling like it wouldn't be enough to conquer the dark entities I was feeling here. "Drive away all harm and fear…only good may enter here."

She called to Archangel Michael for protection and summoned the help of Archangel Gabriel for clear communication, as the smudge stick got passed around and everyone had a hand in sage-ing themselves and the circle as it made its way back to Linda. Around me, I felt a lightness of being, like that of someone kind and gentle, but it could've been psychological or the spirit of my little brother again.

"Billie, if you're here, please go," I whispered. "I don't want you here."

Nothing came to me, and a moment later, the safe feeling was gone, replaced by a heaviness filled with sadness and guilt. So much for sage. I held onto my charm for protection. *Grandfather, please, keep me safe.*

"In the name of the Father, and of the Son, and of the Holy Spirit," Linda said, opening up her towel and pulling out a small cross. She held it up to the ceiling. I closed my eyes. I was Christian—many of us were from years of private schooling—and the prayer felt protective.

Around me, the atmosphere grew heavier, darker. To the naked eye, nothing had changed, but I felt unseen presences flowing through the room like floodwaters reaching every corner. I swore on my life, on my brother's life that when I got back home, I would never mess with the supernatural again. The core of my body trembled as though I were caught stuck in a meat locker. With eyes closed, I felt more sensitive to the energies, so I reopened them.

The camera's red light blinked steadily.

"We ask for protection and implore that any spirits in this home, please come forth and tell us your name." Linda put down the cross and joined hands with Kane to her left and Sharon to her right, as everyone else held hands to form a circle.

For a whole minute, nobody spoke or moved.

The candle flickered gently, though outside was still pouring and rogue drafts blew randomly through the house. The smoke from the sage wand billowed gently, creating a haze in the air above their heads.

"If you can hear me," Linda said, "please come forward and tell us your name."

We waited. I knew where it was. Right in middle of the room. Though I couldn't see it, I felt its hatred. Overwhelming, angry, and now...ticked off that we were summoning it.

"*You...*"

From thin air, a voice spoke in a low, dull thrum. It felt male and old.

I wanted to DIE just like the spirit had asked of us.

The crew all looked at each other making sure none of them had spoken. *Please, God, no, God no, God no...* This couldn't have been happening. There couldn't be an actual male voice belonging to none of us channeling through Linda's lips. I was living a nightmare. Watching Linda, I saw her lips move in time with the voice that was not hers, not anybody's.

"*Get out. Don't you know when you're not wanted? GET*

OUT!"

The voice coming from Linda Hutchinson's lips didn't sound human. I covered my ears, shook my head. *God, please make it stop...* They weren't faking this.

"Why do you want us to get out? If we do that, how will we ever help you?" Sharon wanted to know.

"It doesn't want our help. It wants us *dead*," I muttered, gripping the gator tooth charm.

"Keep rolling," Kane mumbled, one eye on DJ. "You gettin' this?"

BJ nodded, his mouth agape, as he stared forward.

Every single one of the crew members startled and adjusted their seating, clearly uncomfortable. DJ's forehead had broken out into huge beads of sweat, Quinn shook his head angrily, and Kane and Eve exchanged confused glances across Linda's body.

Sharon cleared her throat. "Who are you? Why do you want us to leave?"

No response.

We all watched as Linda's head hung back, her chin tilted into the air, as a line of saliva slowly dripped from her mouth. Slowly, she began to tremble until she was shaking, convulsing, yet nobody would help her. I wanted to leap forward and assist her but did not want to enter their sacred circle.

"Maybe we should end this," I suggested. "She's not well. This isn't right," I said louder. It didn't look right to have an older woman shaking that way with her neck loose, nor to have these people abusing her abilities and kindness this way. "Hello? Anybody hear me?"

Only Eve looked my way, but her expression was one of helplessness. She seemed to agree with me, sympathized but didn't make the decisions, and everyone else was hell-bent on going through with this. I would rather go back outside in the rain. I would rather deal with my own personal demons haunting the woods than this.

"You are not safe here," another voice spoke from Linda's mouth. This one had an English accent, and I immediately knew it could only be that of Gregory Rutherford who'd been murdered here.

"In the name of the Father, and of the Son, and of the Holy Spirit…" Eve murmured, and I crossed myself. "Hail Mary, full of grace, the Lord is with you…" All her catechism came pouring out of her, as she randomly rambled prayers out loud. I was grateful for them.

"Cursed woman…" the first voice continued in its raspy tone. "Leave now."

"We will leave when you tell us what happened here," Sharon said, holding tightly onto Kane and Quinn's hands.

"Cursed woman. It was *you*…"

"Who are you talking about, spirit? Or are you a demon?" Sharon asked.

Spirit, demon—did it matter? There was no body, no face, no eyes, but I felt like he—IT—was talking about me.

"You must go. It's not safe," Rutherford pled with us from beyond.

I felt something surround me, a cold breeze followed by a dark shadow that crossed in front of me and swirled into the middle of the circle forming a vortex that spun faster with every second. The darkness reminded me of the energy I had seen as a child. It was here—it wanted me.

Sharon ignored the environmentalist spirit's request. "Were you murdered? Or were you the murderer? Tell us then we'll leave." Sharon spoke for Linda who was no longer in control, her soul having been overtaken by someone…something. Grabbing the pencil on the table, she again gripped it like a four-year-old might and again scribbled on the bare floor of the house like she had on her crossword puzzle.

"What does it say?" Eve asked, tears in her eyes.

Vulnerable in my corner of the room, I moved closer to the circle, peeking to see what Linda was writing. Sharon shot me a look. I didn't care if my presence was disturbing the energies or disrupting the séance, I needed to see what she wrote.

DIE DIE DIE… Linda scribbled without looking at her words, her body continuing to convulse harder and harder.

CYPRESS
CYPRESS
CYPRESS.
What? No.

"I think we should stop," Kane said, looking at me. His hands still held onto Linda's arm and Sharon's hand.

"Not until he answers us!" Sharon shouted.

Who was the boss here—Kane or Sharon? What the hell was this woman thinking, and why was Linda writing my name? I couldn't hold it anymore and let out tears of frustration that welled up and spilled over.

"Tell us what happened here, spirit, and we will leave! Who are you?"

"I'm out of here." I stood and stepped to the front door. Who would know my name in this place except my grandfather? Could my grandfather be trying to contact me, and this demon wasn't letting it?

"Don't move!" Sharon shouted at me. "It's trying to scare you."

I nearly went back and slapped her. She was nobody

to tell me what to do, especially not now when I didn't feel safe, when I feared for my life. "Yeah, well, it's doing a great job."

"I have forgotten my name," the spirit uttered then shouted, "I won't tell you again!" Nameless spirit opened Linda's mouth wide and from where I stood, a dark cloud of energy emerged from her cracked, dry lips tinged with pink old-lady lipstick. It rose into the air and slammed into the ceiling, knocking a loose beam onto the ground, inches from DJ.

Our screams echoed off the walls, as we scattered. We covered our heads, dispersing and breaking the circle. Enough was enough, and I hated Sharon for forcing the issue when it became clear that we shouldn't have been meddling to begin with.

"Damn..." Kane breathed into his hands, looked away, then breathed nervously into them again. He crouched to the ground and placed his hand on Linda's back, checking her breathing. She had slumped forward, her face pushed into the cracked wooden floor of the house. He pulled her up by the shoulders, checked her breathing.

Limp, motionless.

My stomach gripped around a knot in my core.

Kane's fingers pressed against her pulse points on her neck. No reaction. He pinched the bridge of his nose. "I think she's dead."

THIRTEEN

Yes, she was.

I knew, because I saw it—the familiar soft light rising out of the old woman's body into the ceiling, same as I'd seen the night when my little brother had passed. She was gone—Linda was gone, and we were all to blame.

Especially me.

I hadn't argued with them enough, hadn't warned them enough, not that they would've listened. I'd tried but they blew me off.

"Dead?" Sharon lay her down flat on her back. The woman's body fell limp. "What do you mean?"

"I mean *dead*, Sharon! What the hell else do you think I mean?" Kane shouted, then began pacing in a circle to calm himself down before crouching beside Linda's body again. "Jesus Christ."

Eve threw her arm around her husband's shoulders. "Babe, don't. Let's think about this for a second."

Kane nodded in quick succession.

"Check her breathing, Sharon," Quinn said.

"I already checked it," Kane told her. "CPR...who knows CPR?"

"Nobody. Jesus..." BJ turned his back to us and rocked back and forth.

Sharon tilted back Linda's head, opened her airways and prepared to administer CPR while Quinn attempted chest compressions. There was no point to any of this, because I'd seen her spirit leave. I crossed my fingers anyway, hoping I was wrong and had seen a trick of the light.

They did everything they could do, while Kane and I attempted over and over to get a signal on our phones to call emergency services, but the storm was too heavy and service had been shitty out here to begin with.

Damn. We shouldn't have come out. All signs pointed to staying away, to warning us it was a bad idea, but this was what happened when six stubborn people got together and tempted fate.

Quinn stopped with the compressions, as Sharon stopped with trying to reactivate Linda's lungs. "Lord have mercy," she said, sitting back on her heels. For the first time, she was quiet and resigned. "In the good Lord Jesus's name, Amen." She gestured the sign of the cross over Linda's body. "I can't believe this…"

"What do we do now?" Eve pressed back tears with the palms of her hands.

"That's it. We're done," Kane said. "Let's pack it up, get Linda back to the Indian village or Miami. From there, we'll call an ambulance. Game over, y'all."

"In this storm?" Quinn asked. The man of few words said exactly what I was thinking. It's be better to pack it up and wait, *then* leave.

"What else are we going to do?" Kane asked, his agitation rising once again.

"He's right, though," I said. "We can't go back until the rain is over. Airboats are light. They can't handle conditions like this."

Eve knotted her sweaty locks into a tight bun on top

of her head. "Then we have to cover her, keep her comfortable until the rain stops. Let's pack it up while we're waiting for the storm to blow over. When it does, we leave."

Besides the glaring error that Linda would no longer have a need for comfort, Eve was right. All we could do for now was pack this party up. I watched as Eve held Linda's limp hand and shed tears for the woman.

"Exactly," I said, sorry that it took the death of a lovely woman to realize this. We all looked at Linda's body—a dead body right there in the middle of the floor. A woman we all knew, who'd been breathing and talking moments before, now lying lifeless. It was surreal and nobody would mention the elephant in the room.

Why had she collapsed? What had caused it?

"It was nobody's fault," Kane assured us. "Got it? The situation was stressful. Her heart naturally gave out. We all know she had a heart condition."

She'd a heart condition. *Disease...* Yet they'd allowed her to come on this investigation? Wasn't that selfish and irresponsible, even if she *had* insisted on helping them?

Only Eve and Sharon nodded in agreement. Quinn seemed to think otherwise from his grim thin-lipped stance, but kept it quiet, and BJ was busy rocking himself in the corner, like a mental patient at Briarcliff Manor. "The spirit killed her..." he mumbled.

"BJ, you got something to say, buddy?" Kane asked, hands on his hips.

"I said the spirit killed her," the man said louder, still rocking back and forth. "She warned us to stay away but we kept going and going, then it warned us that someone would die, and someone did!" He was shouting by the end.

"No, bro, that's not what happened. You know damn

well the spirits can't hurt us," Kane said.

"If they can't hurt us, then why do we burn sage?" BJ asked through tear-stained face. "Why is there footage and photos of us with scratches on our arms and backs? Savannah Garden House, anyone?" He'd turned around now and was eyeing the group with anger in his red-rimmed bright eyes. I couldn't remember what had happened on the Savannah Garden House episode. "You say they can't hurt us, yet they do. And now look what happened."

"No, BJ," Eve continued with the theory she and Kane were selling. "She was old, and her heart gave out."

But there was truth in BJ's words. The spirit did warn us that someone would die.

Shit. Shit, shit.

I felt his pain as though it were my own, or maybe I felt exactly as he did, like getting the hell of this island and feeling trapped. There was nothing we could do at the moment, however, and standing around arguing wasn't helping. I stood and charged to the nearest pile of tech gear, lifting random things off the ground and stuffing them in bags.

"What are you doing?" Quinn asked.

"Packing."

"That's not where that goes," he said.

"Then put it where it goes," I stammered, shooting him a severe look. "We need to pack while it's raining so the moment it stops, we can get out of here. If you're not ready by the time the sun is up and the rains have stopped, I'm leaving without you all."

I threw down a boom I was holding and stormed off to find my own things somewhere in this evil house, make sure they were ready to go. I packed Linda's things as well, finding her crossword puzzle and stopped cold.

In the corner of the page, she'd created a beautiful sketch of a young woman. Hair floating in the wind, gauzy dress billowing behind her.

The woman from the woods.

In the opposite corner of the page, connected with tendrils of smoke to the woman in the dress was another woman who looked a lot like me—long, straight black hair loose over my shoulders, medium build, stocky, not very romantic by comparison but just as proud. Hanging around my neck was my necklace with little lines coming out of it as though it emitted power of its own.

I placed the crossword book inside my own backpack to further examine later.

Nobody spoke though everyone had begun moving, slowly collecting things while in shock.

From the beginning, I'd known this was a bad idea, but I couldn't even blame them because I'd gone along with it. I only blamed myself, though I also felt Kane's guilt like a slow fog spreading from his aura to mine. But I didn't want to hear his excuses or pep talk. We had one job and one job only at the moment—to get Linda Hutchinson's body to the nearest hospital, so I could go crawling back to my village to confess the stupid things I'd done. I didn't want payment for my time. It'd be blood money anyway.

Whoever the evil spirit was who'd spoken to us, he still hung oppressively in the room, bearing down his hefty influence, because every single one of us, from the sounds of grunts and sighs and the charging around angrily, acted like we would kill each other if anyone spoke a single word.

I took Linda's sleeping blanket and laid it over her body.

Eve came over and exposed her face in the hopes she

might come back to life and breathe suddenly, but I looked at Eve somberly and covered Linda's face again.

I could forgive curiosity in coming here. I could even forgive letting the old woman come along if she'd been part of the team for a long time, so much that they all overlooked her ailment, especially if she'd insisted. What I couldn't forgive was Sharon's insistence that the séance continue, even as Linda showed signs of physical distress. We should've stopped it while we still could. But we didn't. Because Sharon was selfish and needed what she damn well needed.

The house could take the bitch alive at this point for all I cared.

FOURTEEN

By sunrise, the rain had slowed considerably enough to step out of the house. Quinn and Kane walked over to the airboat to assess the situation. Also to scoop out rainwater using red Solo cups so we could load the boat up and get the hell out of here. BJ, Sharon, and I dragged all the boxes and bags we could out of Villegas House and set up a triage area.

Inside Villegas House, Linda was dead.

A lifeless body covered with an open sleeping bag.

We didn't dare move her. Everyone seemed too nervous to be near her, except for Eve, who wouldn't leave her side and continued to hold the old woman's hand sticking out under the cover.

Had this happened in our camp to one of our family members, we would've cooked for four days as mourning, and part of me wanted to do the same for Linda, but I was not with people of my own tradition, and we'd be leaving soon anyway.

I lingered outside the door watching her still body while Sharon tried getting a signal on her phone.

BJ stood near a tree, talking to himself.

Two hours ago, a sweet woman had been breathing, and now she was gone.

What would we tell her family? Did she have a husband or kids? It made me sad just how little I knew about her. Fifty or so years ago, death had come to my grandfather and others in this same spot. It made sense that the energy of this house wanted more of the same to feed it. This was why my tribe had told me to stay away.

Some houses wanted to be miserable.

Twenty minutes later, Kane and Quinn returned, told us the airboat was ready and that gators had crawled onto the land and piled into a hissing heap.

It was the dead body within olfactory range. We needed to get a move on.

The men all carried the heavy boxes loaded with tech equipment while Sharon, Eve, and I carried the backpacks and lighter items. I heard Kane tell BJ that he'd need to board the airboat first to center his weight so we could load the rest of the items around him. BJ, in massive shock over Linda's death, more so than any of us, lumbered on without a word.

I watched him.

Head down, mumbling to himself. I wondered if BJ had ever dealt with a death before, if this incident might've provoked painful memories of some sort. I could empathize, having witnessed my brother's death twenty-one ago, but BJ hadn't spoken or interacted with anybody in hours.

Watching the boat rock back and forth, we waited until BJ centered himself in the middle of the vessel before piling boxes and bags around him. All that was left was one backpack and Linda's body. Kane wiped sweat from his brow using the hem of his tank top. "Be right back," he said, and we followed him, slapping mosquitos and flinging away sweat.

I hated the idea of driving the boat along the

waterways with a dead body onboard. Traveling in the wild with a body in the beginning stages of decomposition didn't seem like a good idea. We didn't need medical help to confirm she was dead, but I knew we had to bring her to a hospital. Her family would want her body recovered.

Tears had welled up in my eyes thinking about it.

For the last time, I walked to Villegas House, hating myself for having come here and inciting trouble. Once again, I'd survived what someone else had failed to live through. Sharon and I didn't speak to each other, because if she even tried, I would snap at her for being a wench and that would not be good mojo for the ride back. Her life was in my hands since I was the one who'd be driving her selfish ass back to civilization. She needed to be nice to me.

Eve and I stood by while the men entered the house to lift Linda by her shoulders and feet and pull her out of the rotting house. Once they did, they set her on the ground and made room for one or two more of us to help carry her.

"Babe, can you take the last two bags?" Kane asked Eve. I supposed that meant Sharon and I would help him carry Linda.

We each took an opposite side of her torso. It felt incredibly odd to carry a dead woman. Her skin felt cold through her shirt, and it seemed that rigor mortis was already starting to set in despite the intensely humid air.

Taking a last look at Villegas House, I closed my eyes. "Hope you find your peace," I told the house in a whisper. Too much had happened here. Too many lives taken. Too many buried on the property. Now that I'd seen the place with my own eyes, I would never return. Good riddance.

We had taken three steps in the direction back to the airboat when we heard it—the sound of the airboat's engine.

"What the hell is that?" Sharon asked.

"Is that our boat?" I said. Or had someone passing through decided to stop and help us, having seen our boat off the island?

"Put her down, put her down!" Kane barked, and as we set down poor Linda's body, he and Quinn ran off in the direction of our boat. A sinking feeling dropped through my torso. It couldn't have been. He wouldn't have.

Sharon, Eve, and I ran after the men, tripping over our own feet in an effort to reach the boat before being stranded on this patch of cypress for the foreseeable future. When we reached the point where sloughing was necessary, Quinn and Kane, ahead of us by thirty feet, began yelling.

"Hey!" Kane shouted, wading into the water then stepping back out once he spotted the gators. "BJ!"

Unbelievable. He'd done it. BJ had taken off with the airboat, the skiff leaving a heavy wake trail all the way back to the gators making a beeline for our shore. If there was ever a good time to sic alligators on a fellow human, this would be it.

"He left." Eve vocalized what most of us could only begin to process. "He left us."

Quinn pulled forward his shotgun and began shooting in the direction of the airboat, not close enough to hurt BJ but what I'd hoped was an attempt to scare him into coming back. After four rounds, he cocked it back and shot again before it was out. For the first time, I wondered if he had more shells on him. We would need more if stranded here.

"Get your ass back here!" Kane kept yelling. "Not cool, man!"

"Is this happening?" I mumbled. "This is happening."

"Idiot. I knew he shouldn't have come," Sharon said, pacing back and forth, picking up sticks and flinging them high into the trees. "I always knew he'd do something like this one day, weakling piece of crap."

"How did you know?" Eve faced her angrily. "Huh? How, Sharon? Nobody could ever know. Jesus Christ, now we're stuck here." She pulled out her phone but again, the storm created a weak signal, and she slammed the phone onto the ground and stamped her feet. "Damn it! We have no chargers. Babe! We need to call for help."

"Sure thing, honey," Kane said over his shoulder. I could feel a darkness growing in him that wasn't there yesterday or even two hours ago. "Let me just pull out my dead cell phone and charge it using the generator that was on that freakin' airboat, and everything will be great!"

I tried my cell phone too, as Quinn stopped shooting and put the gun back over his shoulder. "I told my family I was going fishing," I talked to myself. "How are they going to find me? They're never going to find me."

"FUUUUUUUCKKKKK!" Kane yelled again, his voice an echo through the trees. He kicked a cypress root with his sneaker then scrambled back onto land, squatting with his hands over his head.

Eve flew to her husband's side, even though he'd given her major shade a minute ago. "He took off. He took off, babe. What do we do now?"

"Where's the nearest place to swim to?" Quinn asked me.

"There might be a gladesmen outpost somewhere, but they move around," I told him. "They wander and hunt. Could be anywhere. Besides, we can't swim here."

"When we arrived, you said we could."

"Six feet maybe. But not far enough to find help. The gators…"

"Then one of us needs to wait here until another airboat passes by, flag them down," Quinn said.

I hated to say it, but unless someone had brought a flare, that was our only option. Waiting for another boat to pass us could take days, a week even. This was how news was made, when teams of soccer players got stuck in cave systems and television production crews got stuck on abandoned cypress islands surrounded by flesh-eating reptiles.

"Unless there's a flare inside one of those two bags?" I asked.

Kane and Quinn exchanged glances like maybe they should've thought of that. They shook their heads.

This was pretty far off the beaten path, but we could always take turns yelling for help and hope that someone airboating could hear us. "You could keep shooting every so often and hope that someone hears us," I said, pointing to Quinn's back. "Did you bring more rounds?"

"I brought a box," he said.

"Was it on the boat with BJ?" I asked. "'Cause only one backpack got left behind with us."

"Was it the one with the ponchos?"

"I think so. It's over by Linda," Kane said. "I'll check."

Quinn sat by the mangroves. "I'll keep watch over there."

"We'll stay with you. It's not like we're going back to the house," Sharon said.

Eve looked at Quinn from her cross-legged position next to Kane. "Actually, the moment the sun starts beating down on us and the monsoon comes back, we may need to get inside that house again. My God, this is a nightmare. I have to call the kids. I have to call them…" Eve broke down crying.

Behind us, Kane held up the box of shotgun rounds while holding the last backpack, and I had to say, I was surprised by how relieved I felt. He came back and plopped down next to Eve to hold her.

Damn Eve, she was right. Until someone rescued us out here, Villegas House would be our only shelter from the storms and beating sun. Between the lack of sleep, stress, and incredible guilt I was feeling, I suddenly felt light-headed and wanted to break down. Eve did, against Kane's shoulder.

Kane hugged her, holding her tight.

Avila…

No.

Avila.

Leave me alone. Unless…

Grandfather?

God, I hoped it was Grandfather and not whatever demonic spirit had taken possession of Linda. I didn't want the same to happen to me as happened to the old woman. If death was her reward for connecting with the spirits, I wanted nothing to do with this "gift," yet the last twenty-four hours had served no purpose except to develop and accelerate it.

Suddenly, it dawned on me—I was the medium of this operation now.

I shook my head until it hurt. "Stop."

"Headache?" Sharon asked.

Avila…

If the dark entity knew I could hear and feel its presence too, would it do the same to me as it had to Linda? It had asked for me. Linda had written my name over and over again during the séance. It wanted me. I was a cursed woman.

"Please stop." I was losing it and knew there wasn't anything I could do about it. In fact, as conditions deteriorated and options waned, I knew it would only get worse inside my head. Feeling overwrought with guilt didn't help either.

Kill them.

"What? No."

"Are you okay?" Sharon touched me, but I shook her off.

"Don't touch me," I growled.

"Jesus, fine."

Around me, it seemed that everyone was starting to lose their shit in different ways. Kane sat on the floor, arms over his head, rocking back and forth the way BJ had done. Eve sobbed, her face pressed against her husband's back, and Quinn paced along the edge of the land just before it dunked into swampy marsh.

"I can't...I can't..." he kept saying. "Can't die here...can't."

"Oh, shut up, Quinn. None of us can die out here. Like you're so goddamned special." Sharon turned and marched back toward the woods. "I'm going to go find a tree to pee on. Screw this."

"We'll have to walk," Quinn said, taking out his gun again and pointing it in the direction BJ had gone with our one and only airboat full of supplies. "I don't want to die out here."

"Nobody's going to die," I said. "Please put that down."

"And you know this because?" He aimed a beady glare my way that sent a chill up my arms.

I had no answer for him. Yes, we may very well die

out here with no food, no cell service, no boat to get back to the village, and an army of hissing gators slowly approaching the dead body. One hope was that BJ would use his good conscience to, at the very least, alert authorities that we needed help once he got back to Miami, or…that he'd come back for us himself.

I kept thinking about my mother. She'd be so worried.

"You're dead when I get my hands on you. Hear me, ASSHOLE?!" Quinn screamed after BJ. "DEAD!" He fired off a couple of rounds into the marshlands. Kane jumped up suddenly and wrestled the shotgun out of Quinn's hands.

"You don't need this right now." He slung the weapon over his shoulder then took off back to the house.

I followed him. We needed to stick together to figure out what to do. If only so we didn't lose our minds. Though with the way I was feeling, for me it may have been too late.

FIFTEEN

A woman was dead, and our only transport off this island was gone.

BJ lost his shit. If he wanted to leave, fine, but why wouldn't he have waited for us? It wasn't like we all wanted to stay and he was the only one who wanted to vacate. I imagined BJ getting to the access road where we'd left our cars and struggling to get off the boat. I didn't care if he slipped and fell into the water, feeding gators, turtles, and fish for days to come. The man had left us in a serious predicament.

Stress piled on us by the minute, tearing at our ability to think rationally.

Kane walked in circles, hands behind his head. The heat was starting to evaporate the rain that had fallen overnight, and clouds of steam rose into the air creating curtains of fog that swirled every time he let his arms drop by his sides.

"I have about eight percent battery left on my phone," Sharon said, tapping her cell and holding it high in the air.

Searching for a signal was pointless this far from a cell tower but she could keep trying for all I cared. Restless, I needed to move and find a solution. I couldn't stay by this house with the gunmetal gray aura, near a dead body starting to decompose. Soon, the corpse would give off a smell, as the day gave rise to temperatures near a hundred. There had to be a way out that didn't involve waterways. It might've involved lots of sloughing through shallow water but we would do whatever we had to survive.

I took off in the direction of the woods behind the house. Maybe I could find an old beaten path for walking the thirty miles home or a discarded old boat.

"Wandering off again?" Sharon asked.

I didn't answer. I didn't feel like part of this team. Maybe I never had, but especially not after the way things were going. I blamed them for our predicament just as much as I blamed myself. I'd let my ambition get the best of me, something my grandmother had often warned me about. Instead of being grateful and staying humble, I had to go looking for excitement, finding death and abandonment instead.

If that wasn't karma for greed, I didn't know what was.

"Avila!" Kane called. "We don't need another dead body on our hands."

I walked on. As I headed for the woods, I glanced over my shoulder to find Kane, Eve, and Sharon all standing next to each other, watching me walk away. I wasn't this callous, but this whole island had changed my temperament.

Kane shrugged before flipping a hand my way, like forget her.

Yes, forget me. And if I found a path back to civilization, I wouldn't share it with anybody. I'd just walk and wade in brackish waters until I made it back. But I knew I couldn't do that, knew I'd end up doing the right thing and telling the others.

I'd never felt so pissed toward anyone before. In fact, it was overwhelming. Something made me want to hurt them, pummel that Sharon to a pulp for what she'd done, tackle Kane for still talking to her like she'd done nothing out of the ordinary. Knowing someone's terrible attitude and doing nothing about it made one implicit in their actions. I held Kane and Eve equally responsible for Linda's death as Sharon.

I wandered through the woods hoping an answer would pop up. Any indication of a gladesman outpost, maybe. A marked trail back home—anything. But the trees grew denser and me without a machete, I had to stop and try a different direction. I thought of the ghostly woman who'd appeared here, the one with red hair who I'd thought was Linda before finding her still alive. The one Linda had sketched in her crossword puzzle. Was she one of the dead buried here?

The soil was soaked and in spots, my boots sank deep into waterlogged holes. The air smelled awful, what with all the rotting leaves, rotting wood of the house, and now a rotting woman just outside of it, the stench of decomposition carried on the wind.

I heard a laugh.

I stopped and looked. Nothing but trees and tangled roots. I checked behind me. Another low laughter rumbled through the trees. I had to be going crazy, one vision at a time. If I wasn't careful, I'd end up a statistic of the Everglades dead. Somehow, I had to get off this land, back home to try and resume a normal life.

"Who's there?" I asked. My voice filled the space and sounded alien.

It had to be ghostly. Nobody walked these woods with me, not in real time anyway. I was the only person for yards in one direction and miles in another.

Another laugh fluttered through the woods, only this time accompanied by another voice, talking to the first, telling him to be quiet, or they'd be discovered. My heart stopped. Blood ran cold. I kept my eyes pried open. I was scared to close them, scared my earlier visions would reappear to haunt me.

Billie, the ginger-haired woman, and the men from the grocery store.

Ghosts everywhere. A slow-moving river full of them.

I'd always known this land was haunted. There was no way people could try to live on this giant waterlogged sponge and not encounter tragedy. Tragedy always occurred where there was water, where man did not rule, where limestone beds absorbed fallen airplanes, disintegrating them, swallowing pirate ships whole that were meant to sail the ocean.

Out here, there were no rules.

And somewhere out there, men were plotting. I heard them, nearly saw them as wisps of energy laying dead animals around the property in an attempt to scare away Rutherford, his wife, and two assistants. The Nesbitt brothers. I had come out here to distance myself from the noise and connect with nature only to find more spirits.

Why me? I was the last person capable of handling visions.

I didn't want to be an antennae for the dead. I only wanted to see Villegas House then come home again. Stupid for thinking it'd be so simple. Now I couldn't walk ten feet without encountering voices from the past.

I stared straight ahead and saw them, fully formed this time—two white men in long pants and undershirts plucking dead raccoons, Snail Kites, and other small animals off their belts and tossing them in the direction of the house. I felt like they wanted to infuriate Rutherford, animal-lover and rescuer that he was, to try and get him to leave. They would stop at nothing until he'd left.

I stepped backwards, a branch snapping underneath my feet.

The brothers paused, looked in my direction. Could these men with shotguns slung over their shoulders see me? But I existed here, now, in another time fifty years into the future.

"Did you hear that?" one asked, slowly taking steps in my direction.

My belly filled with the deep cold terror that comes when you know your luck has run out, and you're about to be discovered. Slowly, I backed away, as one of the Nesbitts took slow steps toward me, sliding his shotgun off his back and moving it into position. My heart pounded against my ribs. I'd felt a less elevated type of fear around white people before, before a racial confrontation, but now it was all too real. He was the hunter, I was the prey. His eyes, bright blue, sparkled with amusement, the thrill of the kill, as he inched toward me.

I lifted my hands in surrender.

Had I slipped into the soul of an endangered animal, or was this exactly as it seemed—man stalking woman? My back hit a tree, one of its spiny branches jabbing deep into my skin. I bit my lip to keep from screaming in the event there was still a chance I could avoid this by keeping quiet.

The man stopped, sniffed the air.

He could tell I was here. In another dimension.

Would that bullet travel through time?

A shot rang out and I squeezed my eyes shut, braced for impact as time slowed. I doubled over, gripping my stomach. He'd shot me. This man had really been able to see me and shot me, but when I looked down at my hands, there was no blood. No pain. Though I heard a scream. Turning, I saw another form, taller than mine, darker skin. A woman stepped around the tree, a thin small brown woman with a gunshot to her stomach, bleeding profusely. She cried out once before falling to the ground, just as the man who'd shot her looked back at his buddy and laughed.

Sick. Bastard.

A moment later, another woman came running through the woods from the direction of Villegas House. Her white nightgown flowed out behind her. "Brigitte? Brigitte?" she called. Upon seeing Brigitte on the floor of the woods, she covered her ears and let out a bloodcurdling scream.

"Gregory!"

He hadn't seen me after all. I wasn't here.

This was Elena Rutherford, and holy shit, I'd just seen a Nesbitt brother shooting one of Rutherford's assistants. It could only mean that he'd shot the entire clan too. I'd just been given a glimpse into time. The man retreated into the woods, silent as a ghost so Elena wouldn't see him.

But I saw him.

And now I knew what happened—he'd murdered that woman right beside me, the iron-tinged scent of her blood still lingering in my nostrils.

SIXTEEN

I tripped over my feet, scraped my knees on the gritty ground before running back to the house because at least other living people were there, and as much as they were on my shit list right now, at least they were real and not trying to kill me. I stumbled onto the porch and heaved.

Sharon, Kane, and Eve surrounded me. I caught the cadaverous scent of Linda's body flaring up in the heat. "What happened? We heard a scream," Sharon asked.

"I heard…I saw…" I began but couldn't finish.

"What? What did you see? Is someone out there?" Kane asked.

I shook my head, felt the lie burn in my chest. "Nobody real. I think I can see…I don't know…" I trailed off. Why should I tell any of them that I could see ghosts? It wouldn't help our situation. A bunch of dead people replaying significant scenes of their lives. None of it would help us get off this island. "Nothing, don't worry about it."

"You can see them, can't you?" Sharon gripped my shoulder. Funny how she only seemed to care when there was something in it for her. "You can see them, just like Linda could."

I shrugged her off. "What does it matter?"

"It matters because there's little written about this house, Avila, and I don't know when we'll ever get the chance to come back here again. You're the only one of us who can tell me what truly happened here."

If I told her about the woman in the woods, the gladesmen shooting Brigitte, my own personal demons out by the water, she would only use me like she'd used Linda. As it was, she had already used me to get here.

"People got killed, Sharon. That's all that matters," I grunted.

"Wrong. It matters who did the killing," she said.

Her voice grated against my eardrum. Why was she so damn insistent? What interest did she have in this whole affair? "The Nesbitt man did. I saw him do it. Just now, out in the woods. There, are you happy?"

"Which Nesbitt brother?"

"I don't know."

"But did he kill everyone? Is that what you saw? Because I don't think he did."

"Back off, Sharon." Kane stepped up to me, setting a reassuring hand on my back. As much as I didn't want anyone touching me, not even Kane, I appreciated his telling her to stop.

"Seriously. Enough already," Eve scoffed.

A wave of undeniable hate rose in my chest. I wanted to reach out and strangle this woman, even though I'd never wanted to strangle anyone in my life, not even the men at the supermarket. "Don't you know when to stop? That's why Linda is dead."

She recoiled like a wounded snake. "Don't you blame me for Linda. Everyone here knew that she was already sick!" Sharon shouted.

"Then, she shouldn't have come," I insisted.

Sharon scoffed. "She *wanted* to help. She came of her

own accord. Ask Kane and Eve since you don't trust me."

"It's true," Kane said. "Linda was happiest when she felt needed and wanted."

"None of this is helping." I growled, holding the temples of my forehead.

"Neither is the pointing of fingers," Sharon hissed.

It didn't matter. Linda was dead and nothing would bring her back. We were here because something about these murders was of interest to Sharon. Did she have family in Florida at the time of the murders? Any other day, I would've been intrigued to know, but right now I only wanted away from this house.

"We shouldn't be focused on the house anymore," I said. "We should be focused on getting home. Has anyone been able to get a signal?"

"Both mine and Eve's phones are dead, Sharon can't get a signal, so that leaves you. You were taking video early this morning when the raccoons broke into our tent. Do you still have battery? Let me see your phone." Kane held out his hand.

I pulled my phone out of my pocket and saw it had 11% battery left on it before handing it over. "I don't get a signal either. We could try walking east as far as we can to see if we can get on the fringe of Miami's closest cell phone tower," I said. "West toward Naples is out of the question—we'd have to swim through the river."

"And those gators are getting closer," Kane said. "I went out there to check on Quinn. They're creeping in."

"They smell Linda's body," I explained. They were braving the evil of the house just for a snack. We had to figure this out. Walking east as far as we could until we hit the edge of cell phone service might've been our best bet, but that was assuming the haunted woods would let us through. I hadn't come back by choice.

"We're going to have to give them the dead raccoon and any other dead animals we find," Kane said, looking at Eve whose eyes were filled with exhaustion and tears. In just a little over a day, Eve had gone from looking like a rich Housewife of Atlanta to a corpse bride, not that I or anyone could blame her.

"What'll happen otherwise?" she asked.

"They'll make their way inland if they're hungry enough," I explained. "Gators have been known to walk into people's homes, swim in their pools, sleep on patios just to find food. They've stayed away all this time—I think they're afraid of the house—but now they're building up courage."

"Because of the body," Sharon muttered, arms crossed and looking out toward the riverbank. "We have to warn Quinn."

"It's easy to outrun an alligator," I told them.

"Run in a zig-zag pattern," Kane spouted off the myth most everyone knew.

"No, just run," I said. "You can outrun one easily, and the best way to do that is in a straight line, because it's the fastest way to get away. Speed outweighs strategy in this case. Let's bring Quinn in. He's been close to the water long enough."

Suddenly, we heard shouts and all turned in the direction of Quinn by the water's edge. Kane took off jogging in his direction. My heart rate kicked up in the hopes he'd come across boaters or hunters in the woods.

"Quinn?" Kane called. "You alright, man?"

The shouting continued, repetitive, as though he were trying to get someone's attention. We found him deep in the woods past the spot where I'd seen my vision earlier this morning. He crouched near the ground looking like a kid who'd found a hidden ant pile under a rock. "Check this out, guys."

Carefully, we made our way through the dense brush to where Quinn crouched in front of a bush. When we arrived and surrounded him, he pointed and we saw what he had found. A small litter of kittens. Panther kittens.

"Cute, aren't they?" He reached out to stroke the soft spotted belly of one kitten. "I heard meowing, almost like chirping, when I was walking this way looking for anything dead I could feed those gators and found this." He petted the kitten again.

"Don't do that," I said, kicking his hand away.

He looked at me with fire in his eyes. "I'll touch it if I goddamn want."

"Sure, put your human scent all over it, so when Mama comes back, she'll know exactly whose ass to kick," I said.

"She has a point, Quinn. Leave them alone," Kane said, backing away. "In fact, we shouldn't even be here. Now we'll attract gators *and* wildcats. Come on. You and me need to go for a walk to try and find cell service."

Stepping over rocks and fallen branches, I made my way out of the woods only to realize we weren't the only ones who'd sensed the kittens in the brush. Two six-foot alligators, bellies on the ground, hissed up at me, exposed pink mouths showing off perfect rows of teeth.

"Okay...nice boy. It's okay..." I stayed calm and talked smoothly like I usually did, but these weren't village alligators who were used to being around humans. These were wild and judging from the way they'd made it inland this far, curious and looking for a snack. "Guys, don't move."

"What is it?" Eve asked.

"Gators. And it's breeding season. Let's try and move

slowly in the other direction."

"Are you serious?" Eve whined.

"Those assholes have been encroaching on our territory all morning," Quinn said from behind me.

"This is their territory, I hate to tell you," I said, keeping my eyes on the reptiles who slowly were accompanied by two more aggressive pals. Now there were four, and more ornery than I'd ever seen any gators. "When I tell you to move, move in the *opposite* direction. They can't navigate through the trees too well."

"Avila? I don't like this…" Eve was crying. "What do we do if one bites?"

"You bite back." I mumbled under my breath, keeping my gaze on the reptiles. "The real answer is gouging it in the eye but with this many to gang up on us, there's a good chance we won't survive, even with excellent eye-gouging skills. So, start walking slowly away. I'll stand here until you're gone."

"What about you?" Kane asked.

"Just go." As the only native Floridian here, as someone who shared territory with gators in the wild and as the most guilt-burdened person among us, I should sacrifice myself.

Just then, one of the gators tired of warning with hisses charged at me. I broke into a run back to the woods, as the others dispersed in different directions, Eve screaming like a child, Kane pulling out the shotgun, aiming it at the reptiles. He fired one shot that stilled one of the gators, just not the one chasing me.

"Run!" I yelled at him, searching for the highest ground possible. There was no point in wasting several shells on animals that would soon encounter trees to slow them down.

But then, Quinn began throwing something at the

reptiles and it took me a moment to realize what he was doing. The second I saw the gators pile on top of each other frantically fighting and thrashing, I realized the horror of what he had done.

"No!" I screamed and climbed several feet up a cypress tree, as another panther kitten flew through the air on its way to becoming gator meal.

"You rather they eat *you*, Cypress?" He reached for the last kitten, holding it high. As he aimed for leverage, the man seemed to take pleasure in his actions. I wished I could say it was pride in his strategy for defending us. After all, the gators were now preoccupied with tearing apart the defenseless kittens, but it wasn't.

It was pleasure in killing.

Quinn didn't look like himself at all. His normally unreadable face took on a more rugged, ferocious appearance. Someone primal, careless, and heartless had taken over him. One of the Nesbitts, down to the jeans and white undershirts, appeared as a transparent overlay on top of Quinn.

I blinked and the double vision dissipated, leaving only Quinn.

Then, I saw her.

She moved out of the corner of my eye.

Leaping from the woods, shiny tan coat without markings, long slinky body rippling with muscle, fierce golden eyes. Ready to kill. She paused, assessing. No roar—Florida panthers couldn't, and that was a shame for Quinn—but make no mistake, she was intensely pissed. In all my years living in the Everglades, I'd only seen the elusive creature once, hit by a car on US-41. This was the first time I'd seen the endangered cat up close in her natural habitat, and I never knew rage until seeing her now.

She watched angrily, as the human murderer of her babies held her last cub high in the air, about to fling it. The cat hissed, teeth bared, nostrils flaring. She crouched on her hind quarters, preparing to spring forth on the unsuspecting interloper. My body pulsed with energy.

I did nothing to warn him.

SEVENTEEN

In the split second it took Quinn to toss that last kitten toward the heap of gators, the cat had pinned him onto his back and torn into his face. Using the force of her massive paws, her claws ripped into his cheeks, goring out his eyes. They hung from their sockets, from the optic nerve, dangling on his cheekbones. His arms and legs thrashed, fighting against the creature, as blood spilled all around him.

I watched, horrified and eerily satisfied.

Screams echoed from the woods, then came frantic debate on whether or not to shoot the cat and risk killing Quinn, but from my vantage point, the damage had already been done. Quinn had stopped moving. The cat had torn an enormous hole into his chest, and his lungs hissed as they leaked air. From my low branch, I clung to the trunk perfectly still, in case the grieving mother thought I had anything to do with this. She paused to glare at me with golden eyes. She didn't come for me.

I felt her pain.

I'd seen it before—in different eyes—the day my brother died.

Even the gators had stopped fighting over their food, paused mid-wrangle, watching the cat, listening to her chirps that belied what should've been furious roars. The panther tore into Quinn's neck, the screams from the woods continued, and finally, a shot rang out, as the mother cat fell onto her side.

I screamed, keenly aware of how odd my cry must've sounded.

How could I explain that while yes, I cared for my fellow human, at the moment, he'd been a murderer of innocent lives? That I felt he deserved his death for callously discarding infants of a majestic endangered Florida cat? A mother watching her children die was still a mother watching her children die, regardless of species.

I looked at Kane, tears blurring my eyes, but then I saw Sharon holding the shotgun. She pushed the butt of the gun into the peat and shot me a glare. The gators dispersed to the edge of the water.

"Don't give me that look. I had to do it."

Florida panthers were shy and wouldn't hang around to torment us. Her reasons for doing so were now gone. I said nothing to Sharon, only watched through an excruciating headache, as Kane and Eve crept closer to survey the carnage. Eve covered her face, unable to bring herself any closer. She stepped into a small clearing and vomited.

I hopped out of the tree, doubling over for breath.

"What do we do now?" Sharon slung the shotgun over her shoulder. I didn't feel any safer with her wielding it than I had with Quinn.

"Like I have a plan? This is a nightmare." Kane coughed into his fist.

"Well, we can't just leave Quinn here," Sharon said. "The gators will get him."

"We can't bring him into the house either."

"Why not?"

"Sure, let's start a body pile, Sharon. Why not?" Kane scoffed. "Great idea. I love the smell of rotting flesh in the morning. Doubling the scent will draw them in faster. Hell to that. We have no choice but to move on. Our kids expect us to come home. I have to get my wife back. Do you see her? Look at her." He pointed to a distraught Eve, sobbing and losing control of her breathing.

"We all have to go home, Kane. We all have lives, but what do we tell Amy when she asks where her husband's body went?"

"We tell her the truth—that we had to leave him behind. There's only so much we can do. End of story. Help me cover them, at least." Kane had begun picking up underbrush, dead leaves, and foliage and carried them over to cover Quinn's feet and legs. One of his shoes had come off, blood seeping out the ankle of his pants.

I staggered over to help Kane, my headache blinding me. I crouched, picked up armfuls of dried leaves and dumped them on top of Quinn's torso, which was partially crushed by the weight of the large animal. About twenty yards away, the remaining gators basked in the sun after the warm meal.

"What about you, Cypress?" Sharon watched us. "What do you guys do when stuff like this happens?"

By *you guys,* she meant my tribe, my people, and her assumption that Miccosukee folks often had to dispose of people expired in the wild due to their idiotic choices was unacceptable. I wouldn't give her the pleasure of a response. All my life, I'd heard questions like these, designed to provoke. Most of the time, I stood against them, but today, I wasn't as strong.

"We dance around the body and pray to the panther gods," I said without a hitch.

"Do you, really?"

"Idiot," I muttered under my breath.

I thought of my mother and grandmother. Even Uncle Bob, as annoying as he could be, wasn't the kind to fight back with words, but if Sharon kept this up, this attitude of supremacy, linked with the stress devastating us at the moment, it wouldn't be long before I had no choice but to kick her ass.

"Very funny," Sharon said, taking off toward the house. "Come on, Eve. Let's find you some water."

This. This was the dark spirit's influence. All of it. This quarreling. It wanted us to argue and turn against each other. It wanted us to fail. What it didn't realize was that we wanted to get the hell out of here just as much as it wanted us out, but now our chances of doing that were even slimmer than before.

Once Kane and I covered up the bodies, he headed to the house while I stayed outside, unwilling to go inside. I'd have to eventually—the afternoon rains were on their way again—but for now, I would only sit outside and ground myself. If I got too close to Sharon, I'd turn into someone I wasn't. And with weird energies affecting us, possibly even causing the tragic events of the day, I didn't trust myself. When Sharon had fired that shotgun, I'd wanted to rip her throat out, and nobody wanted that.

Least of all Sharon.

My headache hammered, a combination of stress and dehydration. For an hour I'd been hearing Eve sobbing inside the house, her husband consoling her, and Sharon arguing with Kane about whether or not he should leave to go find help. I heard them in a detached fog of head pain, like listening from behind a wall from another realm.

I couldn't believe what a massive fail this expedition had been. How it had deteriorated from bad to worse.

Couldn't believe I hadn't listened to my own intuition.

All my life, my instincts had kept me safe, even at the expense of others. If that weren't true, my brother would still be alive today. Why hadn't I listened now? The disappointment that awaited me at home would be unbearable and possibly insurmountable.

I wouldn't be surprised if my family asked me to leave.

To make things worse, I couldn't stop the invisible energies from surrounding me. Facing the house, I could see the aura Linda had talked about, the gunmetal gray atmosphere that surrounded it like a straitjacket. I felt a deep pain between my eyes like my forehead ripping open. In my soul, I knew it was more than a headache—it was gut instinct coming back to taunt me like I hadn't had enough already.

A full-blown attack on my psyche ensued, and I could do nothing to stop it.

I heard crying and arguing, only this time it wasn't Sharon and Kane. It was two other people, and I saw them clearly. An older gentleman on the steps of the house, wearing white pants and a white shirt to deflect the heat. He sported a thick, dark mustache and held a cigar clenched between his teeth. A woman collapsed against the steps in a long light-colored skirt stained with deep red. She cried into her knees, dark hair spilling onto the steps.

I wanted to look away but found myself riveted.

"He shot her," she said. "Just…shot her. For no reason, *amor*. Oh, Gregory. I couldn't do anything to help her."

"Why didn't you stop him?" the man demanded, nervously chewing on his cigar.

"How would you expect me to stop him? You mean

to suggest I could have prevented this?" Her voice sounded irrational and wild, the voice of a woman who'd seen too much and could never be whole again.

"Darling, if this ever happens again, you take the rifle and meet them outside with it. Or better yet, alert me to the problem and I'll do it!" He shouted at her. "Now we have to find help. Come and assist. We have to get her to a hospital before she bleeds to death."

The woman bawled, blubbering about everything being so easy for her husband, because clearly, he had all the answers. She sobbed against the porch railing, while the man kicked a column and disappeared inside the house to fetch his things.

I blinked and tried to shake the vision. I was dealing with enough in present day. But when I reopened my eyes, the ghosts were still there, and there was Villegas House in its earlier days—pretty and cleaned up. Its inhabitants were in a world of hurt. A field of negative energy hovered over them, influenced them, ran unwanted thoughts through their minds. Curiously, the house's aura was gray even back then.

It hadn't turned dark because of the events taken place here.

It'd always been dark.

Something about this island, about this spot, made it that way.

The man I assumed was Rutherford ran out of the house with a bag over his shoulder, preparing to tell his wife something about Brigitte who I saw was lying inside on a bed. That was when another man appeared from the water's edge, along with a little boy of about ten years old. The man was dressed in my tribe's traditional colors, his long hair tied into a long ponytail. The child beside him looked familiar.

Billie. But that was impossible.

He greeted Rutherford and Elena and asked to know what was going on. He'd heard rumors in the camp that continued arguments existed between two families out here and wanted to know how he could help. As a tribal leader of the Miccosukee, ending conflict was his main concern.

My heart pounded inside my chest.

"Grandfather?" Night after night, I'd seen him in my photos. I'd spoken to him and told him about my woes, and now here he was, real enough to almost reach out and touch him.

Rutherford explained that his assistant had been injured and was lying inside the house. His wife had witnessed the senseless attempt at murder, committed by one of the warring brothers, though he wasn't sure which, and he was about to take her back to the city.

"You should not have come here," Rutherford said with a grimace.

"I came because a mediator was needed," Grandfather replied.

"You did so at your own peril. This island is good for no one." Rutherford rushed into the house. From the moment they'd arrived two years before, terrible things had happened, he explained. Arguments with his wife when they had always enjoyed a peaceful marriage. Animals left dead on their doorstep and around the property as a warning to get out. The gladesmen brothers were possessive of the home their father built, a home without a deed, one he had abandoned of his own free will.

The house was fair game, he said. It'd been empty, abandoned.

My grandfather explained how Roscoe Nesbitt had

meant to raise his family there, but they hadn't been able to live here long. The house had been cursed. It was understandable that the Nesbitt sons would feel possessive of the home.

"Well, he was right," Rutherford said. "Because cursed is how I feel."

Then he asked a favor. Would my grandfather be able to stay and take care of his wife and the other biologist, Peter, while he traveled with the injured Brigitte?

"I can do that," my grandfather replied.

The little boy tugged at his arm, as if to argue against staying, but I sensed that my grandfather had brought him as a buffer, hoping his presence would force the two parties to act respectfully and peacefully.

Things moved quickly after that.

At times, it was like watching a movie playing out in front of my eyes, step by step. My grandfather's gaze, at one point, seemed to burn right through me, as though I had caused the problems here. I felt so ashamed, I had to look away. At other times, the blurry visions shifted quickly, like film on fast-forward, and one moment later, Brigitte had been loaded onto my grandfather's dugout canoe while Rutherford pushed off, on his way.

The ghosts moved about at will. At times, they hovered in front of my face, their eyes dark and faces gaunt.

Rutherford's words as the boat drifted down the river: "Keep a wary eye out, old man," he called out. "This island changes you."

My grandfather watched him leave, entered the house, and a moment later, the video in my mind's eye fast-forwarded again then flew backwards. And back. And back in time again. Suddenly, the front yard was covered in still, bleeding bodies. Dozens of them. Some wore traditional Seminole colors, others wore U.S. uniforms of the old days.

They'd been killed in battle, because they'd refused to leave their land and relocate west to Oklahoma. They'd resisted force, resisted bullies. As a result, death had come to these lands. They'd been promised safe haven but the Seminoles knew it was a lie to get them to vacate. In the end, they knew their way of life would never be the same again as long as these foreigners were here to stay.

When I blinked, they were all gone, only a handful of dead lay scattered across the peat moss. One of them was my grandfather. Three other men lay sprawled in poses of sudden death, two I recognized from the woods. They were buried here, all of them. The energy here was intense because they had not rested in peace.

Standing, I shook my head and squeezed the visions from my mind.

When would it ever end? I was ill-equipped. The wrong person to be shown visions of the past. Never had I wanted to be home so much, living my ordinary life instead of this.

Off to the side was a dead body, dark eyes wide open, face and neck bloated and puffy. From the reddish hair, I knew it was Linda, though she'd been decomposing a long time. Her skin was gray, black, and mottled. Slowly, she sat up and looked at me with expressionless eyes, as spidery cracks spread all over her rotting face. She spoke straight to my soul.

Stop fearing your visions, Avila. Listen to them.

Her putrid body collapsed back onto the ground, her head snapped off, and my scream echoed through my mind before my world turned black.

EIGHTEEN

Rotted planks of wood, grains of sand and dirt, and deep grooves covered the wooden floor. It was raining again. And screw my life, I was inside the house again, the house that wanted to kill us. Water dripped in through the ceiling, as someone twisted my face and poured a small capful of fresh rain into my mouth.

"You fainted." Eve's face came into view. "Also, you're dehydrated."

My tongue and throat felt dry, and my forehead felt like it had seized up. Suddenly, I remembered the visions. The battleground, the Seminole, the dead bodies from 1967. I'd suffered another psychic attack, only this one had been mammoth. For what felt like hours, I'd traveled through time in this very spot. Floating above it, not really there but witnessing it just the same.

I had smelled the burning scents of dry land, the sulfuric smoke of warfare.

I'd seen my grandfather, the little boy that could've been Billie in modern times but was impossible since he hadn't been alive back then. I tried sitting up but my head exploded into a field of stars.

Eve held me down gently. "Don't try to get up. You hit your head out there. See?" She swiped my temple and showed me half-dried blood on her fingertip.

The house smelled like shit. It had to be Linda's body. We couldn't keep her here much longer or her decomposition would take an ugly turn with all this heat and humidity. At this point, there was no guarantee we could bring her back either and may have to cover her with dry grass just like we had Quinn.

Two were dead.

Hard to believe since just yesterday, we'd arrived bright and early and tried to make a day out of this production. Less than twenty-four hours later, it had all taken a turn for the worse. It made me wonder which of us would be next and if we'd ever make it out of here. Shock wore off, replaced by anger, exhaustion, hunger. I thought of BJ. If I ever saw that asshole again, I would surely kill him with my own hands.

My nostrils flared from the rage running through me. I had to look up at Eve's feminine features to remember that not everyone in the group had turned out to be a jerk. Not everyone thought only of themselves. Though Eve could sometimes drown in a glass of water, at least she had a nurturing side to her.

"Shh…it's okay, Avila. Keep sleeping. We're figuring out a plan to get out of here."

I couldn't sleep. And that plan better present itself quick.

Because behind her, hovering from the ceiling came a dark mass that swirled but wouldn't take shape. The core, the entity that had spoken through Linda was making its way toward us. Right now, it watched us, observed, attempted to intimidate us, made me feel that rage, even as the others were oblivious to its presence.

I closed my eyes against it. Somehow I had to fight its power over me. Kane and Sharon were arguing again at the far end of the room, a pissing match to drive anyone crazy.

"The moment the rain stops, I'm out of here," Kane lashed out. "I don't care how far I have to walk, but I have to find a cell signal."

"Your phone is dead, Kane."

"I'll take Avila's. It has 5% left. For all we know, the edge of cell service might only be a mile away, and we're here all worried for no reason. I have to at least try."

"So, you're just going to leave three women alone in this house."

"No, you can all come with me."

"It's not safe, babe," Eve said, eyes brimming with tears. For a woman who cried a lot, she held on pretty strongly. Maybe that was the secret. "There could be gators or other panthers. Snakes, wild hogs…" She slapped at her leg. "Mosquitos, rain, lightning…"

"Baby, what do you want me to do? Sit here and pray and hope to be found? That might never happen. By the time any one of our families realizes we've been missing and calls authorities, we could be dead. I can't let that happen."

The dark shape hovering near the ceiling still watched us. Listened. Then, it floated down and swirled near Sharon and Kane. Sharon slammed her hand against the wall, vibrating the weak integrity of the inner wall. "Damn it. There's no way out of this. We're not thinking!"

"Like hell we're not thinking, Sharon!" Kane shouted in her face. "If you think you can do better, then by all means, suggest something. But I haven't seen you come up with a single solution to this situation but you sure as hell are full of criticism!"

"Stop! Can't you guys stop arguing for one minute?" Eve's tears squeezed out of her lids and landed on my face. She continued feeding me small sips of water, as though the action itself were keeping her sane.

Kane rushed over and squatted next to his wife. He drew her face into his hands and kissed her hard and full of determination on the lips. "I'm sorry, but what kind of man would I be if I stayed and did nothing? I *have* to go find help and I *have* to do it while I still have energy."

"Then I'm coming with you."

Kane took his wife's hand. "Right now, we can't go anywhere. But the minute this rain stops, we leave. I'm going to try and doze while I can to save up energy."

The thought of staying with Sharon, just me and bitch-face alone in this house while the Parkers went on a mission to find civilization was not doing my headache any favors. I was too weak to speak my mind, mentally and physical exhausted, emotionally drained and channeling a storm of anger. I hated the thought that now I was one more problem for these people to have to handle.

One way or another, I had to figure this shit out.

For generations, we'd lived in the Everglades and survived. But we had the tools, we had implements, we had each other to solve problems. Here, we had an evil house, rainwater, a shotgun, a bowie knife, and a backpack containing random things.

I wanted to sit up and think my way out of this, but my head continued to pound.

I dozed in and out without meaning or wanting to. I hadn't slept the night before, so sleep came intermittently. After a while, I lost sense of time and had the distinct impression that either Eve or Sharon were dozing off as well, since the steady sound of rainfall and thunderstorms were lulling us all into a stupor.

The dark cloud in the corner of the room was no

longer there. I exhaled a sigh. Lying on my side, my right hand splayed out against the wood of the floor. It was a deep dark wood, so vastly different from other areas of the house that were lighter. Whoever had built the house had used whatever timber they could find, a mixture of different trees, but this wood had a different energy to it.

Yes, energy.

When we first arrived, Linda had pointed it out and even placed a piece in my hand to feel. I'd felt a jolt of power flow through me, which was how she learned I possessed psychic gifts. I'd heard of the ability before, being able to gather information from somewhere else or the past just by touching an object. It was called psychometry.

Between the steady rhythm of the rain, the soft snoring in the room, and the rolling thunder getting farther and farther away, my hand vibrated gently. Before I knew it, my whole arm vibrated, as though it were alive with its own beating heart. This vibration wasn't visible to anyone else, only to me. It reminded me of times when I was young, right before dawn when the energy of the sun would immerse my bedroom and I'd feel like I was floating out of my body.

Something about those still, early morning hours.

Don't move…

The voice was my own subconscious talking. I couldn't move if I wanted to. I was in a trance-like state, my hand pulsating with crackling sensation. After a few minutes, the floor came alive. Moved right underneath my hand, swayed, rocked gently back and forth, the feeling of being on a boat. I was dizzy from exhaustion.

I saw my grandfather's shoes walking along the dirty floor, heard his conversation with Rutherford's wife, as she fought tears while describing what had happened to their assistant. Brigitte had gone out to bring in the traps they'd set up for studying the snail kite, when the Nesbitt brothers appeared, like they often did, only this time they were determined to make them leave.

Depositing dead animals around the property hadn't worked, running their airboat back and forth late at night hadn't worked. Finally, it seemed they'd gotten fed up with their being at the house and shot the first person they saw.

Brigitte had been a warning.

It could've been any of them, Elena said.

Grandfather gave her the bad news that she'd died at the hospital. How did he know, Elena asked. He just knew.

My grandfather had the gift before me, the gift of knowing. Did that mean he'd been susceptible to the energies here, like I'd been? We were more alike than I'd ever imagined. It saddened me that I hadn't gotten to know him in person.

The conversation lingered in my mind. Evil acts had taken place here, sure. These were no-man's lands. Most people knew terrible things occurred in the Everglades and nobody would know any better. It was a well-known fact that bodies were dumped here for good reason, because the earth and water had a habit of swallowing people up, and if the glades didn't get them, the reptiles would.

Murder was an unfortunate byproduct of these lands.

No, what stood out in my mind was the wood my hand still touched, the rocking motion that persisted, and the notion of water and boats and humans who mastered both.

Open yourself, Avila, I heard Linda telling me in a washed-out dream.

The visions served as clues. I'd been here once, long ago, and I'd be here again and again. Our souls recycled. The water, the boats, were a part of my higher self. My grandfather had arrived here that day to help, not on an airboat, but the way all my people had traveled these waterways in the old days—by dugout canoe.

And if we wanted to get off this island…

…all we had to do was make one.

NINETEEN

"What happened?" Kane mumbled himself awake.

"We build a boat. A dugout canoe. That's how my ancestors got around. I can't believe I didn't think of it before."

"And how are we supposed to do that?" Sharon asked, disdain in her tone like she'd already decided it wouldn't work.

I actually understood the process from hearing it explained in the village so many times to tourists. "We need a dried cypress log. There's tons of fallen ones outside. Add fire to burn the cutout, rope…granted, we need a hatchet or machete to carve the shape, so it won't be exactly like a real one, but—"

The words flew out of me. I visualized it in my mind like I did everything else. It'd be something like a dugout, not perfect maybe, but it'd work.

"Where are we going to get a hatchet?" Sharon smirked.

Kane brushed Eve's hair out of her face as she slept. "True, we're fresh out of hatchets and ropes."

"We need to explore the house. We haven't since all this began and maybe we'll find items. At the very least, we can build something to float out of here—a raft or whatever. All we need is to get far enough 'til someone sees us. We have the wood to start. Look at this place—it's falling apart."

"It's true, babe." Eve stretched. "We can pull the rotting wood coming off anyway and maybe float the hell out of here."

"Or the doors. Pull them off, tie dry brush to the undersides, use palm fronds to affix them to the wood," I said, feeling hope for the first time in a while. "We won't know until we take a good look at all we have. What about our backpack?"

I already knew it contained a box of rounds.

Kane got up and headed to the one backpack still sitting by the front door. He opened it and dumped the contents on the floor. The box of shells tumbled out. "There's that. BBQ lighter. One…two…three ponchos. Mosquito repellant. Aaannddd….a bunch of cables."

Orange, rubbery coils spilled out.

I grabbed a cable, pulling it taut. "That's our rope. We can always split it open and use the individual threads if we need it to be lighter. Kane, you have your bowie knife for that. The ponchos can line the bottom of the rafts, help keep water from seeping through." The idea illuminated my brain, the positive thought counteracting the negative vibes prevailing in the house.

"But can a raft hold five people?" Eve looked at Linda's dead body. "One of them lying down?"

I hated to tell her that I didn't think Linda's body would be making it off this island. "Depends on how we make it. Maybe we build individual ones, depending on what we find, and we each float on our own. Our biggest problem right now is the amount of rain and finding dry wood."

"This is crazy, you know that?" Of course, Sharon

had to have an opinion, even though I was willing to bet she'd never contributed a single useful idea in her life. "This isn't freakin' Gilligan's Island."

"You have a better idea?" My heartbeat kicked up a notch. If Sharon could just not speak the rest of our time here, that'd be great. "How about from now on, unless you have a solution to the problem, you don't knock anyone else's idea? Good? Great."

Yes, I was being sassy with *the* Sharon Roswell from *Haunted Southland*, but who cared at this point? She'd shown her true colors, and I was done. My whole life I'd learned that if something weighed you down, you cut it from your life. I was not beyond putting her in her place if I had to.

"I never knocked the idea, Cypress. I only said it was crazy."

My hands shook with anger. Something primal inside of me wanted to rush at her and grab her by the neck. "It's the crazy ideas that end up working and making news, aren't they? It's not like we're trapped somewhere we can't get out. The only thing separating us from home…"

"Is the water. She's right. An airboat's basically a raft with a motor on it." Kane sounded enthused. I couldn't wait to start working with him on getting this done. Finally, a ray of hope in this dismal situation. "How long will it take?"

I shrugged. That was another problem. "Could take days, weeks."

"Weeks? Without food, only water?" Sharon scoffed.

"We can survive without food, Sharon," I blurted. "And we have tons of water, because…" I gestured to the outside world. "I present to you…Florida's rainy season. The problem is finding *dry* wood, we need *fire*, which we can start but it might get put out thanks to the storms."

"And there's no way in hell we're building one inside this bundle of sticks," Kane said about the house.

I stood by the front door and watched the torrential rain come down in sheets. Whatever we built, it'd need to withstand the elements, and it'd need to keep us away from gators. I couldn't imagine a raft that fell apart as we rode along, leaving us impervious to the gnashing of teeth.

A dugout canoe took months to make. The wood had to be carved then dried and baked out in the sun over several weeks. It was simple in design but we were lacking supplies and time. A makeshift raft, however, would work better but could get it get us down the River of Grass thirty or so miles?

"Whatever." Sharon got up and moved throughout the house in her restlessness. "You guys do whatever you want. I think we should hang tight. Someone *will* find us, just like they found those kids in the Thai mountains."

"They found those kids in the Thai mountains because they spotted their bicycles outside the cave system," I said. "We don't have anything to show that we're here. Did any of you tell your friends and family where you'd be this weekend?"

"I did, but nobody knows where Villegas House is. That's why we hired you." Sharon kicked an empty can of beans the wind had rolled into the room and sent it flying.

And when my family realized I was missing, they would ask Kellie for my whereabouts, and Kellie did not know where I was this weekend, because I only told her about the production team hiring me for a tour around the Everglades. I didn't mention Villegas House.

"By the way." Kane held up my phone. "Your battery just died."

"Of course it did," I sighed.

All the more reason to get started.

It was late evening when the rains finally slowed, and Kane wasn't about to go walking in pure darkness.

We'd spent the time scouring the house looking for items we could use to build our raft. In the upstairs rooms, we'd found a dresser full of clothes, old hairbrushes, and hangers. I took the wire hangers, figuring we could bend them into shapes to help tie the wood planks together, but without any tools to chop the planks or wire cutters, the idea would prove difficult.

Another room contained an old wooden table with drawers filled with papers mottled with heavy mold. Sharon spent most of her time here, reading through them, blowing mold around. She discovered them to be Rutherford's research papers on birds, flora, and fauna. She was obsessed with finding a journal, or something that would clue her in as to what happened her, but I was done caring about the past.

All the past had ever done for me was make me fearful.

We'd begun building a foundation inside the house using planks, palmetto fronds, and cables. The house reeked something awful, but we did our best to stay away from Linda's corpse. At random moments, I kept expecting her to sit up and speak to me, so I'd go around exploring cabinets and closets, anything to keep away from Linda.

Sharon would read out loud from Rutherford's observations, as if we cared. I swear, if I heard one more entry about birds and animal eating habits, I was going to roll the papers into a tube and shove them down her throat.

The body's stench got worse throughout the heat of the day and filtered into the upstairs rooms. If nobody brought it up first, I was going to be the one to suggest we move it outside. Whatever happened to it happened to it. In my culture, we didn't make a big deal about memorializing people. We moved on and eventually, people were forgotten. We didn't construct monuments or statues. She'd return to the land, same way she'd come in, though I knew these people's ways were different.

They hung onto everything. Put their people in ornate boxes in the ground. Didn't they realize, as investigators of the paranormal, that Linda's true essence was no longer physical? Her soul had moved on. Left was an empty vessel. I would never say it to their faces, but the body rotting downstairs was garbage and not serving us one bit.

We explored every inch of the house as much as we could until the sun began sinking and the absence of light put an end to our work. I wasn't sure how long we'd been at Villegas House, but I believed we were going on Day 3.

The darker the sky got, the more I feared what would come. Would I see visions again? Would the gloomy cloud permeating the home hover over us again? I felt like it was studying us, watching our every movement, trying to figure out how to make us leave.

Out of the corner of my eye, I kept seeing shifts of light moving in the darkness, orbs flitting back and forth. Some felt harmless, while others felt cold and oppressive. The moment I'd address them with straight eye contact was the moment they'd disappear. Ghosts. They may not have been haunting us every moment of the day, but they were definitely making life harder for us, telling us what to do, as in the case of my grandfather reminding me we came from river-navigating people.

I was using the remaining ambient light from sundown to hunt for tools when a foul smell overrode Linda's and a little boy stood in the doorway to the upstairs hall, blocking my path.

"He's here," Billie said, his dark hair covering eyes that stared out of the two dark shadows of his eye sockets. He stood perfectly still, not looking at me, but past me.

"Who is?" I asked the moment I could breathe again after he scared the shit out of me. He wouldn't respond. "Billie?" My little brother's presence continued to baffle me, since he had nothing to do with this house.

"I don't want to stay. I'm scared, Avila."

"Why are you here?" I asked him. "You never lived here. Why don't you go home?" I felt silly for suggesting he find his usual place to live.

"I follow you," he said then looked over his shoulder and sank into the shadows.

"What do you mean you follow me?"

"I'm always with you, Avila. I love you."

"And I love you." My chest filled with a pain I couldn't process. My little brother had left this life for a better one and the best he could do was hang around the sister that had betrayed him? I wished I could go back in time and treat him better, do it all over again, be the big sister I should've been. Instead I'd treated him like an annoying pest. "Are you my spirit guide?"

He nodded but wasn't paying attention.

I took the chance and asked him more questions. It wasn't every day my little brother materialized in full body right in front of me. As used to his visits as I was becoming, what if I never saw him again after tonight? What if, once I got off this stupid island, the house's effect would wear off?

"Why were you in my vision today?" I asked. "With Grandfather. You were here at the house. I saw you."

"I am not with Grandfather."

"Then, who was it?" I asked, my own answer coming to me in another moment of clarity.

"Uncle Bob," he said.

Uncle Bob.

My grandfather had brought his son with him to Villegas House, to show him how to make peace with others. A lesson in diplomacy. Uncle Bob had somehow survived the murders and came home to tell what happened. My uncle had seen it all. It would explain why he wanted me—all of us—to have nothing to do with this place, why he wanted nothing to do with spirits and ghostly tales at all.

"Your gator tooth is Grandfather's." Billie pointed at the charm around my neck hanging from a leather string. I'd always known it belonged to my grandfather, but I never knew how I'd come into possession of it. "Uncle Bob brought it home."

I touched the charm around my neck.

It was imbued with energy.

My grandfather's energy.

This house's energy.

Which meant the darkness had always been with me.

I'd always worn it, assuming it was a token of the grandfather I never knew, but it was more than that. It connected me to this place. No wonder I often felt immense sadness when my fingers grazed it. Today, I felt the sorrow again, but also resentment that I'd been carrying around pain all my life in one form or another.

Would I ever be free of it?

"Avila?"

"Yes, Billie." I couldn't see my brother anymore. His spirit form had receded into the background, though I could still hear his disembodied voice, I couldn't see his ethereal shape. But I knew he was there, crouching.

"I'm scared."

"Don't be," I told him, though I empathized. I was scared too, but even now, I had to be his big sister. "Scared of what?"

"The angry man," Billie said. "He's right behind you."

TWENTY

I turned slowly.

The "angry man" was the shadow energy shape I'd seen moving throughout the house, only now his form was human. Without a face or discernible features, I couldn't see what he looked like clearly and got the sense that I never would. The spirit felt older, more ancient, like he'd lost his identity over the years.

I held my breath and hoped it would pass right over me.

But the shape floated toward me from the center of the room. I wanted to run but couldn't move. Frozen, all I could do was stand and watch, my lungs seizing breath, my feet rooted to the floor.

"What do you want? Why won't you leave us alone?" I asked.

I could ask you the same.

"You're not living anymore," I tried reasoning, watching the cloud creep closer. The hairs on my arms stood up, as its chilly gale blew over me. "You don't need a home. You can go. Go anywhere you want."

Who decides this? You? He laughed a cackling sound that would haunt me for the rest of my life. It resonated through the house, shaking the walls and my inner core.

A house built with remnants of my own. No one asked permission. They took what didn't belong.

"Because you *died*. The things you leave behind are no longer yours."

Like the talisman around your neck.

I fingered the tooth charm, nearly yanked it off my neck as I finally backed away from the form. Was this activating the unwanted spirit activity all along? I nearly ripped it off me, if it meant not having to see or hear these ghosts anymore.

No, stop, Avila.

Linda's spirit was nearby, talking to me.

It serves you.

It didn't serve me! Nothing about the spirit world had ever served me! And the one time I thought it would was this time I followed a production crew out to Villegas House, and now I was stuck here with them. Stuck in my house of nightmares.

One slow step at a time, I backed into the hallway, the fuming black cloud cornering me. If I tried to run, I knew it would attack me and last thing I wanted was to become the third death of the day. "This used to be my grandfather's but he's no longer here," I told the spirit. "Just like this house should be someone else's. You are the one who needs to leave."

I will not. My home was fractured, hacked, repurposed.

"I'm sorry that happened to you, but you're free to move wherever you want."

I do not nor can I.

"You can if you want to. Accept, forgive, and love. Didn't you love anyone? You can go find them." I tried. I tried words and phrases to reason with this spirit, but I felt its pain and anguish, and it wasn't easy to digest.

My only love was the sea, and I cannot reach her. I am cursed.

He spoke without a voice. To any of the others, I was upstairs talking to myself, yet I heard him clearly in my mind, no English words, just universal language, meaning, thought. And here he was, telling me he'd loved the sea. Well, that made sense for a spirit trapped on a peninsula surrounded by ocean. But whoever he was, he was in pain. He'd done terrible things in life and being stuck in this house was his punishment. He'd paid that price many, many times over and over again through the years.

I wanted to help him. I really did but I wasn't a medium, a healer, or anyone who could guide him. I had my own life to worry about. Besides, this primordial entity didn't want to be helped. He was a demon, a beast now, a spirit out of touch with his original humanity.

"What's your name?" I asked, stumbling backwards further down the hallway.

The entity hovered closer, bearing down on me. It'd pushed me up against the hallway wall, a few feet from the stairwell. I turned my face when I felt it approach, felt the sour breath of rot and decay and salt coming from the misty being, or it could've been the corpse's stench emanating all the way up the stairs. My little brother had disappeared. It hurt me that he had to exist on the same plane as this thing, whoever he'd been in life.

I am no one.

"If you're no one, then you don't need to live here."

I live here because it is no place. No man's land.

No one and no place belong together. We are both forsaken.

"Tell me your name," I demanded. If only I could wield its name, I might be able to guide it out of this dimension. Linda kept telling me not to be afraid, but how could I not when a massive oppressive spirit slowly, menacingly, kept aiming its focus on me?

I am he who rules all who live here—the huntsman, the bird man, your diplomat grandfather—all who dare call themselves captain. There is only room for one *aboard this ship.* Extensions of mist ejected from the sides of the shape and now began encircling me.

Ship? "This is a house, not a ship."

Planks from my wreckage serve as the foundation for this place. A captain must never abandon his ship. Therefore I must stay. There is only room for one. Leave or serve me.

I watched in horror as this shape continued to bear down on me. I felt the choking waters of the salty sea suffocate my lungs, the acrid smoke of his last battle burning my eyes, tasted the blood of those he'd eradicated on the same beams of wood supporting what was left of this structure.

This had once been a ship—a pirate ship.

And the suffering soul was a captain I'd talked about countless times—Bellamy.

For so long, I'd assumed the tale of the pirate ship doomed to roam the Everglades was just a tale, a ghost story to recount around a campfire or an airboat full of tourists at dusk. But legends are born from truth and truths are born from facts. It'd never occurred to me to research and see if Bellamy and the *Vanquish* had been a factual vessel that had sailed.

"Captain Bellamy of the Vanquish," I called on him. "That's who you are."

Blasphemer! Where did you hear that name?

The angry spirit whirled around me, lifting my hair in a harsh tug, raising my feet off the ground. I was rising, being taken, rather, higher up the wall until my head smacked against the ceiling. My skull banged against the wood, and I felt a surge of pain bolt through my spine. One more hard shove, and my neck would split in half.

He was pissed because I knew him.

Undo this curse, wench!

"I can't. I don't know how," I said, gasping for breath. Did he think I was the woman who cursed him to begin with? My vision and lungs choked with smoke and stench. I felt like I'd been dropped in the middle of an ocean battle between ships, and I was being forced to walk the plank while breathing sulfuric acid. But how? Like my other visions, it had happened centuries ago, not today.

I had power over *him*, because I was real and corporeal. He existed no longer and couldn't do this to me unless I allowed it. "You cannot hurt me, Bellamy," I insisted.

Undo this curse, I say!

"Put me down...or...I won't help you!" I sputtered. Suddenly, my body dropped and fell to the floor. The force of my fall ripped open a rotten hole, and my leg sank through the gaping hole down to my knee. In pain, I yanked it out, got to my feet, and stumbled to the stairs. I began hobbling down, desperate to get outside. Where had everyone been while I'd practically choked to death?

I hit a solid real body at the foot of the steps— Sharon.

"Move," I grunted, shoving her. She cursed, stumbled to her knees, then stood again, following me outside. Even the rain felt good, as I tilted up my chin to the sky and felt the very real water pelting my face. Kane had been outside, ripping wood off a weak section of wall and Eve was doing her best to help him.

"What is your problem, Cypress?" Sharon asked.

I faced her. Why the hell hadn't the captain's spirit pestered her instead of me? Clearly, she was the one who thought herself the leader, the captain of this group, so why me?

He thinks you're the Red Witch, Billie said. He was still here. My little brother still lingered, though I couldn't see him.

"Who the hell is the Red Witch?" I asked.

The one in your story—the one who cursed him.

That was ridiculous. How could I be Maria Pilar Carmona, the wife of the Spanish captain who created the curse? I lived three hundred years later and looked nothing like her.

Sharon winced. "Red Witch? What the hell are you talking about?"

"I wasn't talking to you. And my problem is that you have not once tried to be a team player. Instead of asking me what's wrong, you ask my problem. Instead of saying what a great idea making the raft is, you tell us we're out of our minds. It's like you can't stand not being in control."

"This show was my conception, Cypress, or did you not know that? I hired Kane to produce it, but this and every investigation we've ever been on was *my* idea—my stupid crusade to find answers. So, yeah, I *am* in control."

"Well, then you suck at it significantly. People in charge make decisions for the good of everybody. Whereas every decision you've made so far has been for yourself."

Sharon cracked her neck and took deliberate slow toward me. I stood my ground and refused to be moved aside again as the ghost upstairs had done, but the black cloud of energy had widened and spread until I felt like he enveloped the whole house.

"This whole trip was for me, Avila. Kane works for me, Linda works for me…"

"*Worked* for you. Not anymore, you killed her. How many people are you going to sacrifice until you get your answers? What are you looking for anyway?"

"That's between me and the house, sister."

"Then talk to the house, not me...sister."

"You *are* my link to the house," Sharon said. "I can't talk to the spirits like you can."

Two people had died, one had abandoned ship, and she still wanted to talk to spirits. She still wanted to bring the unnatural world into this.

"There's four of us here, Sharon, and three of us want to get off this island. Meanwhile you want to commune with ghosts." I laughed. Of course the host of the ghost show still wanted to commune with ghosts. Just like every ghost host I'd ever seen on TV, they rested at nothing until they got that golden nugget—the holy grail—the full body apparition.

Sharon's nose moved inches from mine. I looked into her steel blue eyes, eyes that would've been beautiful, reflective of a summer sky had there been less anger in her heart. "What did the entity tell you? I heard you talking to it."

"Nothing to do with you."

"*Everything* to do with me!" she screamed, lines around her eyes deepening as her temper grew. She chuckled, caught herself, calmed down. "I need to know what happened here."

"If I knew, I would tell you," I said, doing my best to get away from this crazy woman. I slipped out the door into the refreshing darkness of the outer part of the house to find Kane. I needed to know where the shotgun was without asking him in front of Sharon, but she'd followed me around the side of the house. I needed to feel safe. "Leave me alone."

"Sure I'll leave you alone."

Sharon stopped in her tracks, as though Kane, Eve,

and I had grown an electric force field over the last few seconds. She looked past me. I checked behind me to see what she was looking at. It was too dark to see anything. Shaking her head, Sharon took two steps back then headed inside.

"Holy Jesus," I said to Kane whose shirt was tied around his head. He stopped, wiped sweat from his face, grimacing. "I heard shouting. What's up?"

"What's going on with that woman?" I pointed in the direction of the house. He knew who I was talking about because there was only one highly exasperating woman in Villegas House. "I know she came here on a mission, but the history of this place is now the last thing we need to worry about. Why are you out here at night, by the way? It's pure darkness."

The moment I spotted the good pile of planks on the ground, I understood why.

"It's easier to do this out of the sun." He reached for more siding, wrapping his fingers around the flat pieces of wood and tugging. "Sharon's obsessed. Thought you'd have noticed that by now."

"We're all obsessed about something. That doesn't make it right to harass people when you haven't gotten your way."

"Yeah, I get it," Kane said. "But I also know where she's coming from. She's adopted. Wants to find her birth mother. She's been on a mission ever since someone posted info about Villegas House on that one website—*Deadly Florida*."

The one John got in trouble for talking about on a message board. One little paragraph of information about this house had led her here?

"Wait, what?"

"Sorry, thought you knew. She chose this locale for

our next investigation because of personal connections she has with the house."

"Years ago, Linda told her her father was killed here," Eve added, throwing down a plank of wood. I felt bad for Eve's nails that she was having to do this kind of physical work, but I had to admit it was nice to see her helping. "She went to her for answers, and since then, she's kept Linda close to her everywhere she went."

"Her own personal medium," Kane added.

"Who she used and abused until she got what she wanted." I scoffed, deciding to join in and start pulling wood off the walls. "How much do we need?"

"I'm pulling enough to make a big pile. In the morning, we can assess how many rafts it'll make. Some of this is too rotten to use, I think. We may need to pry off the doors," Kane said. "Anyway, she grew up in Georgia mountains. When she was a kid, she learned she was adopted after she kept having dreams about a woman running out of a house wearing a white dress. A house like this one."

Oh, man.

"Her parents took her to a psychologist who suggested they tell her the truth about her adoption. Ever since they did, she's been trying to find her birth mother," Kane explained.

"Which I can understand," Eve said.

"Sure, I can too, but why would that lead her here?" I asked. "Lots of houses look like this one."

Kane and Eve exchanged looks. "Linda also told her that a woman by your name in South Florida would be able to help her."

"Me?" I remembered hearing this a few days ago, but how would I know anything about Sharon's birth mother? So Linda was to blame for sending Sharon my way.

"Yes, and through her research, she thinks one of the Nesbitt brothers might've been her biological father. Were either married?" Kane asked.

"I have no clue," I told them.

Kane panted, out of breath. "Years ago, she found a photo of this house online and swore it matched the one in her dreams. She's been wanting to find it for the longest time but could never find any info on it."

"Until the *Deadly Florida* website," I guessed.

"Right," Eve said. "And you were the one to take us there."

I shook my head in dismay. "I brought you here and look at all that's happened."

"Not your fault, Avila," Kane said, wiping more sweat. He doubled over to catch his breath. "Not your fault at all. In fact, we were just talking about this. We're sorry for putting you in this position. As producers of the show, we should've told her that this one would be impossible."

"She wouldn't have taken no for an answer," I said.

"So you have figured her out by now." Kane smirked.

I appreciated the apology but couldn't shake the feeling that it was still my fault. If I could get rid of something forever, something that had plagued me my whole life, it would be the irrational fear that I was responsible for everyone's misery including my own.

Had I insisted that Villegas House was off-limits, that there was no way in hell anyone from my tribe would escort them there, we wouldn't be in this position right now.

Some frontiers are better left unexplored.

Sharon appeared around the side of the house like a meek spirit harassed by stronger ones. "I'm sorry for the

171

way I spoke earlier," she said, looking at me. "That wasn't fair of me."

I glanced at Kane and Eve who said nothing, then back at her. Something was up. "No problem," I replied, but I wasn't a hundred percent convinced.

"Could you come with me a minute? I want to show you something."

I stopped mid-pull on a particularly difficult plank that would've been so much easier to remove with the proper tools. Our hands would be shredded by the morning. I gave her side-eye. "I can't right now. I'm busy solving a problem."

It was sassy but I wouldn't follow *that* woman into *that* house again, even if they coughed up a million dollars.

"It's about your grandfather."

TWENTY-ONE

He died two entire decades before I was born.

In fact, my mother was born the same year he was killed and didn't know him either. Uncle Bob had only been a kid, and it was because of him that we had stories about him. They were diffused through the lens of a child, but they were our only connection to him. Him, my grandmother, and others who knew him.

And the necklace around my neck. Every time I touched it, I thought of him, of this house, and the mystery surrounding it. If Sharon had found something related to me through all her rummaging of papers and random items, I wanted to know what it was.

But the gators were encroaching.

In the dark, I watched them creeping toward the house, lured by the prospect of a meal. I wasn't sure how we would sleep at this point, how we would fight them off, how we would even get a raft finished under their watchful reptilian eyes. A vision of us feeding them Linda's corpse struck a chord—if we had to do it to keep them away from us, we had to entertain the option.

Sharon led me into the house, and as usual, I tried not to look at Linda's body but I caught a glimpse of the poncho someone had put over her to help protect her from the rain. Not sure doing so was a good idea, as the plastic material would help trap the heat and gases emanating from the corpse. I was also on the lookout for the "angry man," for the ominous energy cloud now identified as Captain Bellamy. I had nothing to prove it, except that the information had come to me the more my third eye opened to the portal that was this house in the middle of nowhere.

Sharon led me to an area behind the room used as a kitchen, judging from the crude gas stove rusting away in the corner. From the inside of the house, it looked like a closet but just beyond it, it sank a few steps into a secret room. A small window near the top let in just a small amount of light. This house had been built in the mid 50s, early 60s. It would make sense if it were a bomb shelter. Americans in those times feared the threat of nuclear war more than its own systemic racism.

A small desk lay on its side, its carvings intricate and indicative of a civilized person having once occupied this home. One drawer was open, papers spilled everywhere. Sharon bent to pick one up and handed it to me. "More research papers."

"Okay, and?"

"Rutherford wrote tons about daily life. Somewhere here there has to be evidence of my father passing through." She picked up a piece of hurricane lamp glass that had shattered beside the desk. Standing, she placed it in my hand. "Hold this."

"Why?" I pulled my hand away.

"Tell me what you see when you feel it."

"Sharon, no. I'm not Linda. I don't have a handle on this yet."

"Please just do it."

"I'm not a performing monkey, Sharon. Just because

you snap your fingers doesn't mean—"

"Just do it!" Sharon shouted then bit her bottom lip in a failed effort to calm herself. "I saw you holding that wood that Linda gave you. I saw the way you reacted. I watched your hands spread all over the floor right before you woke up to tell us about carving a boat, and I know you keep that gator tooth around your neck to remember your grandfather."

"You don't know shit about me."

"That's where you're wrong. Linda told us so much about you before we even met you."

"Why? How would she even know me?"

"She didn't. It wasn't her job to know anything, just to relay information. To tell us what she sees, what she feels, what she knows…" Sharon still held out the broken hurricane lamp. What did this have to do with my grandfather? Nothing. She had lured me in. This woman was not to be trusted.

"I can't stay here." I turned to leave, but she reached out and grabbed my arm.

"You and Linda both could see things attached to objects. Just hold this and I'll be done, Avila. I swear to God. Just do it. Please."

I stared at her eyes in the darkness, a light within them, imploring me. Like Kane had said, she was a woman on a mission. Adopted. Haunted. More than the homes she investigated. I guess if I had one chance to find answers related to my birth mother, I might act a little crazy too.

"I can't see visions in everything I touch. Look, I know you came here with a goal in mind, but that goal has changed and every minute is of essence. We need your help out there, and all you're doing is exploring this house."

"It's changed for you, Avila, but not for me!" She shoved the glass into my hand. "Hold it. Please." Her bright, pained eyes demanded, and something inside of me told me I needed to comply.

Sharon was not right in the head.

My eyes bounced around, searching for the shotgun, knowing I'd feel a hundred times better if I knew it wasn't anywhere near her. When I didn't move fast enough, she pressed the glass into my hand, drawing blood. "I said, do it."

"Bitch. You cut me," I growled, yanking the curved piece away and slamming my elbow into her chin.

Sharon gripped her chin and gave me a demented smile tinged with blood. "I'm going to forget you did that, because I need you. *Concentrate* and tell me what you see."

"Shut up," I said through clenched teeth. "This is the last parlor trick I do for you. After this, I'll be getting the hell out of here."

She said nothing but I caught the ire in her eyes, the determination to make her time here worth every minute, even at the cost of others. Sharon Roswell, doing what she did best—using others.

I breathed in deep and let it out slowly to ground myself. I let any thought run through my mind, whatever it may be, and out of a jumbled mass of worry and fear, I imagined this room as it'd been fifty or more years ago. This office, bomb shelter, or whatever. Fifty years ago, that small window facing east had been open. The morning sun shone through it, though it wasn't as hot as it is today. A cool breeze wended its way into the subterranean room.

A set of slim fingers curled around the edge of this desk.

A woman gripped the edge, lurched forward, then lurched again.

Her arms rigid, her face like the surface of the river on a clear morning. Young, beautiful with dark hair falling over her cheeks, as her hair moved in agitated waves. She held on tightly, a swatch of fabric tied over her mouth and knotted behind her head, as a man stood behind her, wide hands gripped over her hips. She'd been instructed not to make a sound, and even now as she looked at me, or appeared to, she couldn't ask for help. Even though her life depended on it. The knife blade against her neck promised her that.

Over and over the desk lurched forward, an inch at a time.

My lungs felt constricted, my pulse quickened, and I thought I might be having a heart attack. I released the glass and it fell, shattering into even smaller pieces on the wooden floor. Shards disappeared into the rotted holes of the wooden flooring. "Get that thing away from me."

"You idiot. I can't believe you broke it. What did you see?" Sharon yanked my hand down toward the floor, placing it on the desk. "Tell me. The faster we get this over with, the faster I'll help you outside."

"You mean you won't help until you've gotten what you wanted?" I fought her grip on my arm. I never expected a woman like her to have this much strength. Glaring at her, I said, "You might never know. You may as well *get used to the idea.*"

"I *will* know, one way or another."

"You won't if I don't help you," I said. "And with those gators headed this way, you'll be the next one dead. Once you cross over into the spirit world, you'll have all your answers." It hadn't meant to come out as a laugh, but it did.

The next thing I knew, Sharon Roswell, host of the TV show *Haunted Southland*, had slapped my face with the back of her hand. "Cheeky little shit," she hissed.

My cheek stung. A fire flared inside of me.

Hold it together, Avila, I thought. *This woman is not well.*

It was better to give her what she wanted and quietly slink away than to fight. If I struck her now, we might never get off this island. Kane and Eve would be dealing with two more dead bodies.

"Just tell me what you saw."

"A woman," I spat and hesitated on how much to tell her. Something told me this was her mother. But this was it—this was what she wanted. Better to get it done and out of the way. "She was raped in this room. I think it was one of the assistant biologists," I lied.

What if telling her the truth angered her, made her worse?

"Who was raping her?"

"I don't know." Another lie. It was one of the Nesbitt brothers, possibly her father. I hadn't seen his face, not that I would've recognized him, but I didn't have to. I knew he was a Nesbitt from his camouflaged pants and dirty undershirts, the shotgun strapped to his back, same way the brothers had appeared out in the woods where they were buried.

"You're lying to me. Tell me who it was."

"It's like you want to hear that it was your father. Is that what you want me to tell you?" I yanked my hand away from her and stumbled to my feet. "It was one of the brothers, I don't know which."

She stared at me then shook her head. "Do you know why we're here, Avila?"

"Because you dreamed about this house. Kane told me." ,

She smiled. "That's right. Because I dreamed about this house every night during my childhood. All my life I've been searching for photos of it in books, on the internet, even articles on microfiche, never finding it. You don't even know what microfiche is, do you?"

I watched her laugh for a whole thirty seconds. I didn't know what was so goddamn funny.

"You fucking millennials. You wouldn't survive without mommy and daddy to do shit for you. My search has led me to hundreds of houses, hundreds of locations for our shows. But never this one—never the one I actually needed to find. Then, finally, last year I find *one* photo of it."

"On the *Deadly Florida* website," I said.

"That's right. So now I'm here, after a lifetime of searching, fifty-one years old, Avila, and you want me to just give it up, accept it, move on?" Sharon grabbed my wrist and twisted it, slapping the piece of glass back into my hand. "I'm not going to *get used to the idea*. Try again. Who is the man committing rape?"

As someone who knew exactly where I'd come from, the history of my people given to me every day by my elders, stories orally crafted and lovingly delivered, I felt for Sharon Roswell—I really did. I felt sorry for anyone who didn't know their origins and I was grateful to know mine. This woman had been searching for her parents, and my touching this stupid piece of glass could give her the missing piece she'd always needed.

So, why did my body warn me with every fiber of my soul?

I closed my eyes.

Again, I saw the woman, her face clearer this time. Crystal blue eyes shone from a pale face, as she realized someone was in the hallway, someone who could help her if only they could hear her all the way over here in the bomb shelter. Her assailant paused, pulled away, and stood on his toes to see out the window. She cried out through the gag, prompting her rapist to slap her, press his blade to her ear.

"What did I tell you? No noises."

Seeing him clearly now, he was definitely one of the two men out in the woods who'd shot the assistant, one of the two brothers fighting to get this house back. The knife he used to threaten her had etch marks on the side—W.N.

"William. It's William Nesbitt," I croaked.

"Bill," Sharon whispered.

But it wasn't so much the rapist who stood out to me, it was the victim. Bill Nesbitt hadn't raped the assistant biologist—this was Elena Villegas with the pleading eyes and the rag stuck in her mouth. I'd seen her in the other vision crying on the front steps when my grandfather arrived to help.

"What are you doing here?" Bill paused, fixing the waist of his pants and coming around the table the moment he saw me. I dropped the glass and moved away, sure as hell that this ghost from the past had noticed me watching him committing a crime.

He was coming for me.

"Get away," I said.

"There's nobody here, Avila," Sharon said.

But he was—he was coming for me.

I ran from the room, positive that Bill Nesbitt had seen me watching him—witnessing his crime. Running down the hallway, I looked for a way out, felt Bellamy following me, laughing. I was supposed to be watching her, keeping her safe while her husband was away, only her husband was back now—just outside—and his wife was here with this man.

What was happening?

I looked down at the shotgun in my hands. Hands that were darker, wider, and more wrinkled. Hands that were not mine. How had this appeared?

This was crazy. When had this shotgun appeared in my hands? Who was I, and why could I only think about the rage I felt? The pure anger coursing through my veins, the resentment of having been tricked by a wicked woman, condemned to the sea of grass forever. I wasn't Captain Bellamy, and yet Captain Bellamy lived inside of me.

I tried shaking the images from my mind to no avail.

My thoughts weren't my own; they were someone else's. I was trapped inside the mind of someone else entirely—and now I knew who. My fingers clutched the gator tooth necklace around my neck. My grandfather's. I was supposed to be keeping Elena Villegas safe, but instead, I'd been outside with my boy, and as a result, this animal had sneaked in and assaulted her.

I lifted the barrel of the shotgun, even though I'd never shot a man before, and aimed it at him. At the offender. Fury flowed through me at both him and his brother. Wrath at myself for not doing my job, the one job I had promised Rutherford. The other Nesbitt brother stepped into the house at just that moment, met in a hallway and both of them looked at me, pleading to give back the gun.

Rutherford announced his arrival, demanding to know what was going on. I felt the fury within even at him for having moved into this house, for not having left the premises when trouble first started. Because of him, a woman had died at the hospital, a family wanted their home back, and a spirit possessed this home, even me.

Now they would all DIE…

"Mr. Cypress, sir. Don't do this," Bill Nesbitt pleaded, hands up. "You don't want to do—"

I pulled the trigger, heard the screams.

Multiple shots.

In every direction.

Watched them fall—both brothers—slumped to the floor. A pool of blood spread throughout the rooms and hallway. I shot again. All of them, every last one of them—Rutherford, the male assistant, Peter, who'd come out of his room to see what was going on. All their faults. I wouldn't even be here if it weren't for them. The biologist's wife watched in horror as I murdered the entire outfit—both warring parties. I could not shoot her, as she'd been my charge to protect, and the boy I would spare, because he was my own flesh and blood. But I had to end this reign of terror before I caused more harm.

I turned the gun on myself.

What had I done?

Oh, God, what had I done?

TWENTY-TWO

"Avila!" Sharon shook me so hard, I held onto the handrail to keep from tumbling back into the small room. Bomb shelter. Wherever the hell I was. "What the hell?"

Kane and Eve rushed into the kitchen and found us at the steps leading down.

I panted, gasped for air, reality, and all the sanity I could find. I pulled at my hair and sobbed full sized tears. I wasn't Robert Cypress, my grandfather. I was me and it wasn't 1967. What the hell had just happened?

"My grandfather…"

"You were screaming." Eve caressed my hair.

"My grandfather…"

I couldn't say much else. The words felt stuck in my throat. The blood—my God, the blood was everywhere.

He committed the murders. But that was impossible. My grandfather had been a peaceful man, a diplomat, a tribe council leader, for the love of God. He'd come here to mediate, to make peace between the feuding families. He hadn't come here to kill anyone.

I needed space, to sort this out, and so I stumbled through Kane and Eve, through the kitchen, on a heat-seeking mission to find air and space. I felt claustrophobic. It was impossible. Impossible.

"No, it's not. It's not…" I rambled incoherently. Exhaustion and emotion welled up inside of me. I didn't know what was up or down anymore. Without sanity, I would never get out of here. I was already halfway gone.

"Avila, tell us what you saw." Sharon reached me, sidling up to me and grabbing me by the arm, whirling me to face her.

I shoved her off and her back hit the wall. "Tired of your demands. Leave me alone."

"No, listen," she insisted. "If my father didn't commit the murders, then I need to know who did."

I couldn't help sneer at her. "You need to know, you need to know. Your need to know everything has ruined our lives. He didn't commit the murders," I growled. "Now, leave me alone."

"Who did then? You saw who did it, didn't you? I heard you saying, 'What have I done?' Who did it, Avila? God damn it, stop walking away from me!" Her fingernails dug into my arm.

Ripping my arm and cocking it back, my fist came pummeling forward with a mind of its own and cracked into the side of Sharon's face. If I made it out of here alive, I would deserve an award for dealing with this woman, the house, and the psychic attacks I never asked for.

"My grandfather."

Sharon stood, shocked, hand to face, staring at me.

I stopped in the hallway and gaped around the living room.

At Linda's dead body.

At the rotting, festering walls dripping with rainwater.

At the black cloud of hatred and cursed death seeping through the walls.

At the pools and pools of dark liquid spilling from

innocent veins.

I couldn't shake them off, the images.

Grandfather Robert Cypress had walked into Villegas House—cursed, haunted Villegas House—after taking a slow walk with his son, my Uncle Bob, and found Elena Villegas getting assaulted. The guilt had consumed him at first, and then a wave of rage had risen over him. Because the crime he was witnessing had been his fault, to some extent, for not watching over her, sure.

But none of that had been the real reason he'd snapped—the real reason he'd snapped was because his spirit had been taken over by the oldest entity here. Same reason why Roscoe Nesbitt had vacated the house ten years before. Same reason why nobody had been able to live here in fifty years. Because Bellamy had been a cursed soul, first in life, then in afterlife, condemned to ruin the lives of everyone he came across until his curse was lifted.

He possessed the body of whoever was in charge, and for some reason, he thought that was me.

"Your grandfather killed everyone?" Sharon's mouth was agape.

"Not everyone." I spoke into the wall as more visions came to me. They were everywhere. I couldn't escape them. The only way they would let me go was for me to leave their influence. Until I could do that, I would never be free again. "He spared my uncle who was a child then. And Rutherford's wife."

I looked at Sharon.

Same heart-shaped face, same eyes as the woman who'd been raped.

"Your mother."

"No," she said slowly. Blue eyes pierced mine. "No, Avila. My mother was a Florida gladesman's wife, Bill Nesbitt's wife who's still alive and living somewhere in

Big Cypress. Linda told me Nesbitt was my father, but first I had to find out which Nesbitt brother…"

"No, Sharon."

"Yes. It's just a matter of narrowing it down, and besides, she couldn't bear to raise a child alone without her husband, so she gave me up for adoption. See what I mean?"

My head shook slowly.

I stared at her.

She had it wrong. "I'm telling you. Your mother was Elena Villegas of this house, wife of the English avian researcher, Gregory Rutherford. It's why you're drawn here, why you've dreamed of this home so much, because of the trauma imprinted in your soul the day you were conceived."

The words flew out of my mouth, the information coming to me through a portal that had opened up inside my higher self. Streams and streams of information, all by touching these walls, this necklace around my neck, by looking into the mind of this woman.

I wanted nothing more than to get off this island and close this portal forever.

She stared at me with blank, disbelieving eyes. "So I'm looking for the wrong woman."

"Yes."

"Then where is she?" Sharon asked. "Where is Elena Villegas then? Wasn't she murdered here too?"

"Your father raped and impregnated her. My grandfather shot him when he realized what he had allowed to happen, then went crazy and killed everyone else, including himself, out of guilt. He spared your mother. She left the house, bringing my uncle back home with her. Nine months later, she gave birth to you."

"Where is she?" Sharon was losing patience. Every

moment of the last fifty-one years of her life was hinged on this one.

I breathed out slowly. There was no other way to tell her. "She committed suicide the same day as your birth. I'm sorry, Sharon."

Sharon absorbed my words like a fish out of water desperate to breathe again. Her gaze would not move from mine.

I bent over and breathed to avoid heaving.

I felt sick with guilt, with knowledge I wish I had never received.

All my life, Uncle Bob and the tribe had been telling us to avoid Villegas House, telling us it was evil. Uncle Bob had remembered his father as a martyr, but he never told me he'd been there the day of the murders. He'd been there. And he'd *seen*. He'd witnessed what his father had done with Nesbitt's shotgun. He'd even taken my grandfather's gator tooth necklace back home with him as a memento. Why had he given it to me?

All these years, Uncle Bob had lied about what he'd witnessed.

Lied about the truth of Villegas House, but why?

To keep our honor as a people, otherwise, what would others think? What would officials think? What would government think? Fear, so we wouldn't lose our benefits. Fear, so we wouldn't be relocated. Fear that we would lose respect for our council leader, for a man with an immaculate moral record. To preserve his reputation.

Only it'd been a lie. ALL OF IT.

My grandfather hadn't been an honorable man who'd been caught in the crossfire, killed by gladesmen out for revenge, like everyone had rumored. My grandfather had been possessed by the evil spirit of this house, had murdered people in cold blood. Maybe that made him a victim himself, but the facts were still the facts.

A murderer lived in my past.

And I wore his charm around me like a talisman.

"I need air." I stumbled toward the front of the house, past the rotting, decomposed body of Linda Hutchinson. Outside, a group of gators stood hissing in the rain, asking for handouts. I screamed at them, wild angry animal to wild hungry animals, mouth wide emitting all the rage I felt.

They continued to gape, mouths open, minus the hissing.

"Avila," Sharon called from the front door.

I turned and faced her. "What now?"

Just looking at her, I saw through her soul.

Elena Villegas Rutherford had escaped the horror along with my uncle, taken him down the river back to the village before disappearing. Where she had the baby, I didn't know, but Sharon had been adopted by a nice family and raised near Atlanta. A life of wanting to understand her roots had led her here. Whether I'd learned all this through psychometry or through Linda Hutchinson who had somehow passed her knowledge onto me before she died, I didn't know.

I didn't want to know.

"All my life, I was scared that my father had been a murderer. But now you're telling me he didn't commit the crimes. Your grandfather did."

"He committed *a* crime, Sharon. Rape is a serious crime, in case you didn't know. Because of that, Elena gave birth to you. Because of rape, she couldn't handle life and checked out. These are the impressions I'm getting thanks to you making me touch objects I didn't want to touch."

"Aren't you glad you know the truth?"

"Not especially. You?"

"I'm alive because of your grandfather. But Nesbitt didn't kill anyone—your grandfather did, and that takes a burden off my back."

"And places it on mine. Thanks for the reminder. That's what I needed right now," I said.

"You know what this means?"

"What?"

"You're the one we should watch out for." She pulled up the shotgun and cocked it. "All this time I thought it was me, thought a curse lived in my veins. But it's you we need to be careful of. You we need to get rid of."

I slowly stepped away. "You're crazy, you know that? I'm not a killer."

"You're not? You have all the makings of one. You're wracked with guilt, you live in the Everglades where it's easy to dispose of bodies, murder runs in your family…"

I backed into a gator who snapped at my ankle, setting off hisses from the other gators. I kicked the lunging creature in the eye. The gators all stumbled into each other, forming a heap, as I jumped to avoid their teeth.

There was no denying that Sharon had lost her damn mind, but part of me wondered if she was right. With all the rage I'd been feeling, I could snap at any moment, and the first one I'd come for was her.

"Come back here, Avila."

"Enough of this." Kane tried wresting the gun out of her hands, but she shoved him down the steps and he tumbled onto his back.

Sharon took aim and fired off one shot that grazed my shoulder. I dove for cover, ending up in a thicket of trees near the bodies of Quinn and the golden panther. The smell reached my nostrils. Around me, two snakes slithered off in protest.

Eve shrieked and cried from the corner of the room, and Kane, back onto his feet, slowly made his way up the steps toward Sharon. "Listen to yourself. There's no proof that a curse passes on through generations."

"She walked in her grandfather's footsteps, Kane," Sharon said. "I watched her. I heard her talking through her grandfather's spirit. Don't we see this all the time? You want to wait and find out after she snaps? You want to die? Because it's Avila causing these deaths. Open your eyes."

"You are out of your goddamned mind," Kane said. "Maybe her grandfather was already angry before he did this, maybe the entities here didn't help. Maybe the builder of this house was already angry, too. You can't just go and blame Avila because she's related to him anymore than we should've blamed you for being the daughter of a murderer."

"But he wasn't a murderer. You heard her."

Kane took slow steps toward her. "He shot a woman, Sharon. A woman who died later on. Put the gun down," he ordered, moving closer. "None of Avila's visions are facts anyway. The past won't matter to a jury when you're in jail. Put. The damn. Gun. Down."

But Sharon continued to aim out the front door in my direction, as gators debated between rushing at Kane and getting too close to the house they reviled. She'd lost it. The biological mother she'd sought all her life was dead. Had been since the day she was born.

She would not be meeting her on this trip.

Also, because of the deaths of two of her crew, because of being trapped here, because of the endless rain, because of the revelations, because her tormented life had led her to this moment, because of the ghosts...

The reasons didn't matter anymore, only the facts. Sharon was our enemy.

Sharon's finger was on the trigger, and that was reality. I'd felt the temper within me too, but I hadn't pointed a gun at anyone.

I closed my eyes and imagined Kane swiping the shotgun from Sharon's hands.

A moment later, I heard the struggle unfold. As Eve screamed and covered her ears, Sharon and Kane grappled for control of the shotgun. Had I caused it? She kicked him in the groin but he fought through the pain, crumpling, knees buckling but still fighting for the gun. Both his hands twisted and pried the shotgun from her hands, and as they both fell to the ground, kicking and fighting.

Eve reached into the melée and yanked the shotgun from Sharon's hands. I watched it all—this house of madness.

"You're making a mistake," Sharon yelled after her. "She'll take it from you. I've kept my eye on her since she arrived. She's been wanting that gun, Eve, honey."

I stepped out from the shadows, hissed at an approaching alligator. Grabbing a stick off the floor, I jammed it into its snout, as I walked by. The reptile retreated back to the group. It would take more than alligators to scare me today.

"I never wanted the gun. I wanted it away from her," I clarified. "For this exact reason. So crazy bitches like you couldn't touch them."

It took all my power not to kick her face in as I approached. She'd been cut on her forehead from scuffling with Kane who gasped for breath and had broken out into waterfalls of sweat all over his body. Eve backed into a corner holding the shotgun. "Give it to me.

I'll put it somewhere safe," I said, holding my hand out.

"Don't give it to her," Kane ordered his wife and shot me a glance.

"Are you kidding me? I'm not the one to mistrust here."

"I don't know that," he said. "None of us can be trusted at this point."

That was true. None of us were in our right minds, especially not Sharon who stood, helped Kane up with an outstretched hand then promptly punched him square in the face. "Asshole," she mumbled.

Kane reached out to grab Sharon, but she'd moved away, stumbled toward the stairs, and rose into the shadows, straight into the overhanging cloud of darkness that awaited her.

TWENTY-THREE

Not only had the gators arrived at our doorstep, but so had turkey vultures. They'd been circling above the cypress trees since earlier today, and now they'd landed in search of their treasures. Without a front door, they'd soon walk into the house and find themselves a meal.

I walked into the house as though floating through a dream.

Bellamy's oppressive mist had grown, now taking up most of the house. I felt the darkness the moment I stepped inside. We were all under his influences—me, Kane, Sharon, even Eve. As long as Sharon didn't take possession of the shotgun, the situation was still manageable. Though Eve held the gun, and Kane had his bowie knife, I had zero ways to defend myself.

Just as I was about to climb up the stairs, I heard movement to my right. I paused, one hand on the railing and looked over. Linda was sitting up, the sleeping bag and poncho fallen over to one side. Her exposed upper half was gray and black, her eyes bulged out and her tongue pushed out of her mouth.

My heart literally stopped beating.

From her corner of the room, her head twisted toward me.

She's up there. Waiting for you.

"Who?" I asked, my voice shredded by fear. Sharon? Yes, that was why I was going up there. One way or another, Kane, Eve, and I had to handle this situation.

The witch, she said using no voice whatsoever, but I heard her clearly. I was horrified by the sight of the old woman, rotting away undead. *The Red Witch.*

My feet stumbled on the first steps, as I slowly backed away from Linda who continued to stare at me, stench emanating from her. Yes, she'd been a nice lady in life but I didn't want her staring at me, sitting up, or looking like she wanted to walk the way she did right now. This house and everything within was doing this. Torturing me.

I tore my gaze away and slowly ascended, following the sounds of Kane and Sharon arguing, checking back frequently to make sure Linda wasn't following. They were upstairs in one of the front rooms where a chair lay on its side and a pile of dirty rags sat in a corner. The sun was starting to dawn over the darkest night of our lives, but it was only the beginning.

Eve stood in the corner holding the shotgun, as Sharon encroached on her slowly. "Sharon, listen to me," Kane said from the door to the room. I stood at the other door to the same space, keeping my eye on Sharon. Four of us stood in four corners. "I get it. We've been through a lot, and we're all going a little cuckoo for Cocoa Puffs."

"Understatement of the month, Parker," Sharon mumbled.

"But we need to hang in there. We can't get at each other's throats. We can't lose our shit. That is what the house wants. Do you hear me? It's what it wants. We cannot lose our composure," Kane said. "We have to focus on getting out of here. So, let's all cool down and take a step back."

"If she gives me the gun, everything will be alright, Kane. Tell your wife not to be an idiot. I've always known she was useless to the production team, but now she's taking it to a new level."

Kane feigned a scruffy laugh. "Sharon, I ought to drag this knife straight through your back for that. But I won't. Because I know you're talking from a place of stress. Baby, don't give her the gun. Do not…give her the gun."

Eve had taken to crying again. "I can't take this anymore. I don't know what's happening to us. Kane?"

"Baby?" Kane approached slowly like four live bombs were about to go off. "Like I said…we're losing our minds, but you've gotta hang in there. Whatever you do, don't give it to her. In fact, hand the gun to me, baby. Hand the gun to me."

But Sharon had walked Eve into a corner, and the poor woman shook like a shivering, wet mouse. "Stop. Get away from me, Sharon. I swear I'll shoot you."

"Let me do it, honey," Sharon said, holding out her hand. "Let me save you the trouble and do it for you, for all of us. It's the best thing we could possibly ask for right now."

Eve's tears ran down her cheeks. With eyes swollen and shut, she shook her head, holding the shotgun like a teddy bear, arms crossed over the barrel. God, I wanted to jump in and grab it from her then run the hell out of the house away from all these people. "This is all so pointless."

"What is, baby?" Kane asked.

"All of this. We're going to die out here anyway. It was a mistake to come here. I told you but you wouldn't listen," Eve cried, turning her cheek into the wall, smearing her tears into it. "You wouldn't listen."

"This isn't the time to be pointing fingers, Eve," Kane said, keeping his distance. From Sharon's peripheral vision, he mimed the action of shooting at the ceiling to Eve. Eve did as he asked and fired off a round right into the ceiling. Wood chunks spattered in all directions. In fact, I'd never seen a time when Eve didn't do as Kane asked, and she cocked the gun and warned Sharon with another round. "Stay away from me."

If Sharon had reloaded the gun, that meant there were three, maybe four, left inside.

"Give me the gun, Eve. Or better yet, turn it on yourself."

"Shut the hell up, bitch. Are you even listening to yourself?" Kane said.

"She's lost it completely," I told him, as I stepped closer to Sharon from her left side.

Sharon swiveled her neck to give me a look. "Says the girl on the brink of killing us all. The girl who learned the truth about her grandfather. The girl who walks in his shoes." She lunged at me, ripped off the gator tooth necklace and tossed it across the room, laughing when another blast rang out.

Eve had shot the ceiling a third time. Pieces of wood splintered and rained to the ground, as dust exploded everywhere.

"That's enough," Kane told his shaking wife.

Sharon covered her head but still reached out a hand toward Eve.

"We're going to die anyway," Eve blubbered. "Let her finish us."

"No, Eve!" Kane yelled. "That's not you talking. That's the house, the demon within these walls! You said nothing of the sort when we were outside working on the raft."

"I know, but I can't...I can't take this anymore." Eve sobbed. "It hurts too much. Please let her end this pain."

"Smartest thing I've heard all day," Sharon said. "Let me do it so we can all die quick."

"No." Kane rushed at Sharon who rushed at Eve. He shoved her aside, pushing the flat edge of his bowie knife against her neck, pressing its point into her jugular. "Don't freakin' move. Babe, give me the gun." He pried the shotgun from his wife's trembling hands and aimed it into Sharon's laughing neck.

"Look at us. And not a single camera rolling." Sharon's eyes squeezed shut as she laughed over and over again. "We finally have a scrap of real drama worth putting on TV and nothing."

Just then, we heard it—a voice.

A woman's singing.

We turned toward the source of the sound but found the hallway empty. Shadows covered the walls and floor and ceiling, and I felt Bellamy's ire with every breath I let into my lungs. I hated these people. Hated them with a passion for being self-serving, for not listening to me in the first place, for insisting we come here and letting it get to this.

I wished I had Kane's level-headedness to recognize that it was the madness inside of me doing the thinking, wishing we'd all be dead, so this could end. But I felt the pain with every cell of my body, even as I knew I was under the influence. Felt Bellamy's years of isolation, humiliation, and penitence for the wrong deeds he'd committed. Felt Roscoe Nesbitt wishing his wife and two teen boys would be dead. Felt Rutherford slowly losing his mind in the isolation of studying the *Kahayatle*.

"Who is that?" Sharon twisted to look.

The woman's voice came from deep within the walls,

from the ceiling, from the ether. I knew her voice as though I'd heard it in my dreams, and maybe I had. Maybe I'd heard it a thousand times as I'd told the tales, maybe I'd even invited her into my life and now she was here. The woman Linda said was upstairs waiting. The same woman I'd seen out in the woods and on Linda's crossword puzzle sketch.

The woman with the fair skin and red hair.

A long green dress curled through the walls before I could even decipher where she was coming from. Her hands were tied behind her back and she sang a Spanish lullaby as though nothing were wrong, as though she weren't walking to her death. Because she was. To the edge of the ship, ablaze with fire and heat. A crimson tangle of smoky tendrils she was, with her orange hair kicking dust into the air like a fiery Medusa.

She looked at the wall, or at Eve, a sad, resigned smile, like we would soon understand her fate. The angry man bellowed through the house. I knew we all heard him, because everyone, even Kane and Sharon, especially Eve, cowered upon hearing his booming voice. He shouted, *And ye be the last to die, wench!*

No, she laughed under her breath. *For all you've done, for your sins, you will roam the glades forever, trapped in a sea of grass. I'll have the last laugh, captain. Aye-aye.*

And she floated through the room.

We watched her in awe.

Each of us, all of us, witnessing the specter's full glory, full-body apparition, the holy grail of ghost hunters right here in wicked glowing splendor without a camera to capture it. She was beautiful to watch, horrific because this would only end one way, and because I knew her pain. He'd killed my husband, my one and only love. And for that, he would pay. An eternity would not be enough for his sins.

I felt her pain.

I knew her pain.

I *was* her pain, because I'd known her long ago.

She danced to her own rhythm in this room frozen in time. Where we each were, I couldn't say, since I floated and swerved in a darkened room tinged with sunrise in time to the woman's singing. Transfixed we were on the ball of orange light moving through the room, singing a Spanish lullaby.

Duermete mi niño, duermete mi amor...

We were satellites orbiting around her. The wife of the Spanish captain, the witch who'd cursed Bellamy forever. Her soul had moved on, but now she was back for one last appearance on her way to walk the plank, or perhaps she did this every morning, replaying out her fate for the empty glades to see. What a lonely existence.

Transfixed in her presence, we froze while she made her way to the window.

Duermete pedazo de mi corazón...

Dream sweet piece of my heart.

I had brought the woman home.

Through centuries of rebirth, the Red Witch was me.

The gunmetal aura of the house deepened, so much that it was hard to see anything else except the scene playing in front of us. Taking invisible steps to the window, the angel of death turned and pointed her gaze right at me, silky, torn, green threads billowing behind her as though moving underwater. I saw the space where her ear should have been, where it had been cut off and fed to the reptiles. Her dress was soaked with blood dripping from the side of her head.

I felt the pain on my own skin, the searing burn of cut flesh.

This ship is diseased with wrath and greed.
But you will break the curse, Avila.
How?
How can I break the curse?

Of course, she wouldn't tell me—she wanted Bellamy to rot in hell forever. But I felt it now. Yes. I had come to Villegas House to undo the curse and release the souls within it. It had taken death, it had taken fear and my grandfather's tragedy to finally bring me out here. The necklace around my neck had been made from the animal that had refused to extinguish the Red Witch's life—a crocodile, not a gator. The crocs too frightened to come near her. Imbued with her energy from the waters of her drowning, it had allowed the continuation of her soul into everyone who had ever found it on these sacred lands.

On the shores of Florida Bay, someone had found it and relocated it to the Everglades. My grandfather had worn it before me and several others before him, including an unwilling soldier on the battlefield of the Second Seminole War near this spot. They were all inside me. I was the ongoing result of many lives.

I was Miccosukee, I was American, I was Spanish.

We were all connected.

Calmly resigned to her fate, the Red Witch walked through Eve, seemed to bring her along. Her naked feet stepped over the edge of the precipice, and then she was gone.

In my suspension, I floated to the window to look out and see where the captain's wife had disappeared to and found her falling slowly, timelessly down toward the alligators waiting below. The stench of death mixed with salty seas and the ferrous scent of spilled blood filled my nostrils, as the house ebbed and flowed back and forth, rocking over invisible waters.

Bellamy shouted, his voice shaking through the ship.

He'd lost his fortune, lost his chance at appeasing the king, lost half his crew in the fruitless chase. And now, because of this damned woman (everyone knew that women were bad luck aboard a ship), he was forced to leave this house. Screams filled the home, of anger and rage that seemed to last forever, ancient fury that would never see completion. This ship—this house—was an endless trap of grief and would always be unless we burned it to the ground.

Burned it to the ground.

That was what I needed to do—burn the infernal thing down.

The Red Witch knew but hadn't told me.

But I knew anyway.

Because the Red Witch had *been* me—long ago.

The entity moved through the room, charged out through the ceiling, blasting a corner of the roof open, and the darkness lifted slowly. We found ourselves back in the present, wondering what the hell had happened. Sharon's back was pressed against the wall out of utter fear, Kane's mouth hung open wide, soundlessly, his breath lost on the last of Bellamy's curling, pervasive shouts.

I'd traveled through a dream back in time.

Eve, though—was gone.

"Babe!" Kane's shouts echoed through the empty house. Had she slipped out while the ghost woman in red had captivated us? "Babe! Where are you?" Kane ducked into the hallway to search for his wife, but my gaze remained transfixed on the window.

This house made of pirate ship wood made you feel its pain, forced you to walk its footsteps, feel the throbbing agony of all its fallen, slain, and cursed.

I knew where Eve was.

TWENTY-FOUR

My hope was to confirm what I already knew and to get to Eve before her husband saw her. I ran to the window and there she was twelve feet below, broken body on the ground below, torn by alligators. They wrestled over the meatiest pieces at the meal that had dropped from the sky. As we'd watched the woman in red, transfixed, it'd been Eve who'd stepped to the window, Eve who'd cast her last words, Eve who hadn't been able to handle the stress.

"Shit." I closed my eyes.

"Babe!" Kane continued to call for her.

"Kane…"

I didn't know how to tell him. This moment, caught between normality, if we could call this moment normal, and the instant where your life changed forever, this moment charged with electricity.

"What? What is it?" His eyes filled with understanding and he flew to the window, pushing me aside by taking up space. His gaze fell on what I'd seen, and the wave of terror and unspeakable dread I felt emanating off his soul crushed me.

"Kane…"

"Oh, no. God, no. No, no, babe......no." Kane sank to his knees, the gun slipping to the ground and resting beside him.

I tried, like any fellow human, to console him, but what do you tell someone who's literally watched their wife get torn apart at the seams by animals of the earth doing nothing other than being animals?

"I don't know what happened. We saw the ghost...the ghost came in the room..." I tried putting together coherent thoughts, but there was nothing to say. No explanation that would bring her back. Words mattered as much as running down to save Eve.

"She wanted to die," he cried into my shoulder. "I felt it."

"I did too."

She did. She'd been losing her ability to cope faster than the rest of us. I had seen it in everything she said and did. What little emotional strength she had, she had because of Kane keeping her together, but Eve, from the beginning, had not been fit for this excursion.

"What happened?" Sharon asked from her spot, back still pressed against the wall. Still in shock from the ghostly encounter, she looked at us with the energy of a dying vine.

I shook my head at her and held Kane's shoulders as he sobbed. The man's energy leaked from his pores. He was dying as I held him, maybe not a physical death, but a spiritual one. There was nothing left to live for, try for. Everything he ever did, he did it for Eve. He wailed like a wounded animal, a sound I never cared to hear ever again. If I ever made it out of here alive, that was.

As his broken spirit disintegrated in my arms, I thought about where we'd go from here, how we'd ever find the energy to finish building that raft now that he almost certainly wouldn't want to anymore, and then something slipped from between us, creating a pocket of air alerting us to its displacement.

The shotgun had moved, slid along the floor, and was now back in the hands of Sharon Roswell, its barrel pointed straight at us. "Sharon…" I pleaded, holding up my palms in surrender. "Haven't we been through enough?"

Her eyes were filled with resignation. "We have. Every moment of my life has led me here, to this house, and this is how it ends."

Ends?

"No. Listen, this is the only the beginning," I told her. Wasn't sure what I meant for her exactly, but she needed to hear positive words, something that would inspire her, remind her that we were all connected. Surely the words should mean something to her personal story. "Sharon…"

Slowly, she got to her feet, still aiming the shotgun at us, hands trembling. For the first time in days, she looked human. I almost agreed she should kill us out of mercy.

Almost.

With every step closer, she pointed it more at Kane. I wracked my brain trying to figure out a way to swipe it away, to jump at her like the panther had jumped on Quinn, to move faster than the speed of light and knock the gun from her hands, but we were at her mercy. And being at the mercy of a woman going mad was to die a painful death.

"It's better this way," she said. "Right, Kane?"

To my shock, Kane nodded, his cheek brushing against my shoulder. He'd lost his will to live. In my arms, I held a dead man.

"No," I told him, hoping my shake would snap him

out of it. "Sharon, no. We'll move on from this. It's traumatic, but we'll find a way. Life goes on, finds new meaning. Sharon, don't..." I thought of my mother sitting at her table in the village, talking to tourists on a Sunday, not realizing I wasn't home yet. Or realizing it and worried to death. It was Sunday, wasn't it? Unaware that her daughter was caught in a house of hell miles away. I thought of my grandmother, my uncle, my little brother, of the life I'd led.

It'd been a good one.

Even with all I'd complained about and all the guilt I'd carried, it'd been a good one. My grandfather's had been too. The American soldier. Maria Pilar Carmona's had been too.

But I wouldn't die today.

The shotgun blasted, the force sending Kane backwards in my arms. I looked at the bleeding hole in the middle of his stomach, at the life force leaking out of his gaze, and my lungs filled with fury again.

So, we were doing this today after all. This bitch and I would be fighting to the death, because screw this woman if I was going to let her take me down in her whim of miscalculated insanity. She would not have the upper hand, not if I could help it. From the beginning, she'd thought she'd been the head of this whole expedition to hell, but I had news for her—this was *my* territory.

With one last pulse of energy left in him, Kane whispered, "Get her."

I charged at her with full force, knocking her against the wall, pushing the length of the shotgun up under her chin, choking her with it. In my mind's eye, Sharon's eyes bulged and her tongue pushed out and she died right here, at my hands, but her knee jumped and caught me in the groin.

Motherfu—

We swapped places at the wall and then I was the one with the weapon under my chin. Our strengths felt about the same, a surprise considering she was older. But she was also more fit than I was and it showed. Her pressure on the rifle against my chest was excruciating, the tension in our tangled arms faltering. We could break at any moment, but I wouldn't.

I kicked her hard in the knee, and as she cried out, I stumbled out of her grasp and headed for the backpack in the corner of the room. A can of mosquito spray. If I could reach it, I could blind her. She shot at me and I ducked, bulldozing into her midsection, head down, as she shot again.

At this point there had to be zero shells left in the damn thing.

Taking hold of the shotgun, I wrestled it out of her hand and threw it against the wall, watching it bounce off and land near Kane's limp hand. His body was still twitching in agonizing death. Chest heaving, gasping for breath, Sharon charged at me.

"You could've shot me," she said, slamming me, knocking me down. "Why didn't you?" A punch slammed into my face.

"I'm not a killer." Running out of strength, I reached and flailed, catching my fingernails on her face and tearing off little strips of skin.

She screamed as she hit me again, ramming her fists into my face over and over. I began blacking out and knew it would be a matter of time before I couldn't see anymore. From somewhere behind me, or maybe above me, or within, I heard laughter—the captain's laughter, the "angry man." Bellamy loved this, lived for this.

As my eyes swelled shut, I spotted my little brother in

the middle of the room, disappointed that his big sister was a lame fighter who couldn't end things in a big wicked witch way. He wanted to help any way that he could, and then—he did.

The backpack slid across the room. Reality felt warped, time slowed down, and Sharon and I rolled on the floor, fighting for the upper hand. At one point, I was the one above Sharon, glaring down at her, focused on the bruises forming all over her face. Our shoulders had tapped Kane's, and she had reached out and snatched his bowie knife from his belt. A second later, I felt searing pain in my shoulder, as the blade sliced through, jagged edges ripping away at muscle. It burned, and I blacked out for a moment, falling onto my side, gripping my shoulder.

Any moment now, I'd feel the knife again, this time in my chest.

I waited for it, expected it, even cocked my knee back, ready to kick forth if I had to fend her off. My hand rested lightly on the backpack, but I'd already forgotten what was inside. I could focus on nothing. All that was clear to me was a violently angry woman poised to kill me, the mad laughter of a scorned pirate echoing through the house, and my little brother trying to shout through dimensions that silenced him.

Get it, Avila.

Billie, I'm sorry. I'm so sorry you were taken.

So sorry I couldn't save you.

It should've been me.

It should've been me in the front seat.

My grandfather stood in the room too, watching me lose this fight to the woman who'd used me to get here. Taken from me, taken from Linda, taken from everyone, and for what? Truth? Had that truth given her peace?

Truth had only given her permission. Permission to act like the animal she always was, only now she had a legitimate reason.

The only way to win this would be to kill her, and I could never do that.

I wasn't my grandfather, and I wouldn't let Captain Bellamy win over me.

That only left death—my own.

The bowie knife whooshed down, straight for my chest, but I blocked Sharon's hand with my arm, heard bone crack. Whether hers or mine, I wasn't sure, though I felt blinding pain spread through me again. I was made of pain at this point. In my hand was the can of mosquito spray. I'd pressed down on the nozzle and was shooting her face with the mist.

She stepped back, tripped over herself and fell to the hole-riddled floor.

"Damn it. Why? Why would you do that?"

"Sorry, not sorry," I said.

Using what little strength I had left, I dragged the backpack closer to me and fished my hand around for the barbecue lighter. The minute Sharon rushed at me again, I was on my feet, gaining my second wind. I slapped her hand hard, knocking the knife out. It slid along the floor, whirling like a fidget spinner.

Pressing down on the trigger, I turned on the lighter.

"Don't come closer," I told Sharon whose hands were pressed over her eyes. She stumbled to a stop. "Fair warning, there's a lighter in my hand and a can of mosquito repellant in the other. If you come closer, I'm torching your ass."

If I did it, I'd be no better than my grandfather, the man who murdered a slew of people in this house in 1967. I'd become a victim of the curse, and I'd only prove

Sharon right.

Walking backwards, I found the bowie knife again, jammed it into the can and watched the flammable liquid spray violently into the air. I covered the walls, the doors, entered the hallway and covered the handrails of the stairs. Covering everything I could until the can ran out, I stood there with the lighter in my hand, its flame flickering and ready to set this house on fire.

Sharon managed to open her eyes to a squint. "Go ahead, Cypress. Burn the house with me in it. You'll end up in the news as the Indian woman gone mad, responsible for multiple deaths out in the Everglades."

I laughed hard. And couldn't stop.

I would.

And it would be worth it.

TWENTY-FIVE

"Nah."

The voice was not mine, nor Sharon's, nor any ghost's from what I could gather.

Our attention was brought to the man on the ground, coughing up blood.

"It'll be the Black man who finally got tired of all this shit." Kane's fingers curled around the cold metal of the shotgun and a moment later, a shell ripped open Sharon Roswell's forehead. She dropped to the floor into a puddle of her own life force.

It was done.

I rushed to Kane's side, guilty for not having tended to him sooner. Always with the guilt. I would live with it my entire life, wear it like a badge of honor. "I thought you were dead."

"Go. Burn this motherfucker to the ground."

I pulled up his shoulders. "Let's get you out of here first."

He groaned through intense pain. "I'm done." His breath was laced with finality.

"You're not done. Let's go." Me pulling and tugging at two hundred pounds of solid muscle did not go well, and Kane's head lolled to the side. I lifted his face and tapped his cheeks. "Hey…hey. No, you don't. Kane…"

There was no reply.

I did it all. I pumped at his chest, took off my blouse and pressed it into the bleeding wound of his torso, happy patchwork colors compressing death. I pumped his chest again and blew air into his trachea. Nothing.

I was surprised to find myself resting my forehead against his chest and sobbing pitifully, as though I'd known him personally. I hadn't. But what it had taken most people to learn about another in a whole lifetime, I'd learned about Kane in two days. If I ever got off this island, I would remember this man as my friend.

I cried for what could've been.

I could have been friends with Kane and Eve. I could've moved to Atlanta and started a new life. I could've gotten to know their adult kids. I might've worked in production, and they could've taught me things about myself that I never knew. But it wouldn't happen now. And their kids would never see their parents again.

Holding him against my chest, I raised my face and screamed into the newly risen sunlight. How dare the sun dawn on this mess, revealing the carnage and chaos we'd fought so hard to avoid through the night? It came anyway. It came because some forces were not to be messed with, and Villegas House was one of them.

The warnings had all been true.

I breathed in deep and touched Kane's face. If Eve were here, I'd touch hers too. I'd link her fingers entwined with her husband's and back away slowly, leaving them to rest together, saying my goodbyes and offering pitiful excuses of regret. I was sorry, sorry for having accepted their offer. Sorry for having brought them here. Sorry for believing that things might go better than expected, that good might prevail over evil.

I'd been naïve.

Five people were dead.

Grabbing the backpack, I gave the dead one last look, offered a silent prayer, even for Sharon, who I could forgive—she had not been in her right mind—and backed away. I lit the walls on fire, the door, the handrail before descending the stairs, heard the booming shouts of Captain Bellamy, telling me not to go in his wordless language of hatred. His job was not done, not until we were all dead, and as much as I felt the pull to stay and let myself burn in this house along with the rest of the team, out of guilt, out of fate—I wouldn't.

Linda wouldn't want me to.

Kane and Eve wouldn't want me to either.

I would finish what we started, one way or another.

While the house slowly burned from the dry inside out toward the water-soaked exterior, I worked on the raft, pulled together pieces and tied them with electrical cable. I sliced the outer plastic coating with Kane's knife and used the thinner wiring to make the frame lighter. Every now and then, I'd look up and watch the plumes of smoke climb into the air, flesh and bone and souls rising up with it. My only hope was that the smoke would alert local gladesmen or tribe members or researchers working out in the *Kahayatle*.

Anyone who otherwise might not think to come this way.

If I got out of here alive, then Kane and Eve's efforts would not have been in vain.

It took two days for the bulk of the soaking wet house to burn, the same number of days it took me to finish building the raft. I tore planks of wood off the burning house with bare hands, tied more planks together with cables and dry palmetto leaves, drank rainwater, slept with one eye open, braided dry cypress fronds for more rope, and tied plastic ponchos to the underside to create an extra layer of protection against water seepage. I found several good sticks for wading through the grass and sucked blood from my shredded hands.

On the third day, the house burned to the ground.

Charred black remains smoldered in the heat.

When police would ask why I'd burned the house down, I wouldn't be able to say it was my strategy for breaking a curse so I'd tell them it was my only defense against wildlife. Because of the fire, the stench of rotting flesh had shifted to cooked flesh, and the gators had moved back into the water in search of cooler temperatures. This was the only way I was able to drag the raft into the river.

A girl had to do what a girl had to do.

Kneeling on the raft, holding onto the wading stick, I watched the last of the house burn down. Two center walls finally collapsed in what had been the living room, and the orange, scorched pieces erupted into columns of ashes and smoke.

Goodbye, Kane.

Goodbye, Eve.

Goodbye, Linda and Quinn.

Later, Sharon.

Quinn had long been digested, and BJ—God only knew where that POS coward had gone. Watching the house burn, I drifted away slowly, knowing there would be peace on this land from now on. With no one to disturb it, no crazy humans to set curses or go mad in solitary confinement, nature would soon reclaim her. Tranquility would once again reign supreme.

The blackened remains drifted out of sight, and the

ghosts of all who'd walked this land waded with me. The production crew, the avian expert, Rutherford, his wife, Elena, the man who'd raped her and fathered Sharon, the assistants, my grandfather, even my Uncle Bob as a child.

They followed me down the river.

Past the fields of sawgrass.

Past the mangrove tunnels and rows of anhingas stretching their wings to dry in the morning sun.

We passed the upturned wreckage of the airboat. Of course it would spill. BJ didn't know how to maneuver the skiff, and he'd had the balls to take off and maroon us during a rainstorm, no less. Of course karma got him. Gators did too. There was no way for an inexperienced man like him to survive this. I stopped and tried to recover items, but the boat was upturned, and heavy tech equipment boxes were of no use to me on my lightweight raft anyway.

I had zero energy. I had to lie down.

The sun beat down on my shirtless body. Floating through the morning brightness and heat in just my bra, I heard my little brother's airy voice telling me to hang on just a little while longer—I was almost there and shouldn't give up now. In fact, he'd already alerted Uncle Bob in a dream. He and other tribe members had been notified of a non-brushfire blaze and were on their way up the river.

Okay, Billie. I love you.

I felt a deep sense of peace but also sadness. What messes we humans made.

I thought of Captain Bellamy, of the Spanish witch who wouldn't go down without a fight who'd cursed him to this very last day. Me, in another life, I was certain. We were all connected in a cycle of life and death. I wondered if the captain was with me now, too. After all, a captain never abandons his ship, and this raft had been fashioned partly from his own vessel, the *Vanquish*.

They say that on dark nights when the moon is only a sliver, you can see still see the doomed pirate ship sailing along, searching for a way out, its ghostly crew trapped in a prison of watery grass... I looked up and saw the waning quarter moon. I laughed at the irony.

History repeated itself.

Only Bellamy wasn't the captain now.

I was.

Acknowledgments

No book would be complete without acknowledging the fine people who made it possible. I would like to thank Iretta Tiger, LaVonne Rose, Houston Cypress, and Mercedes Osceola of the Miccosukee and Seminole Tribes of South Florida for contributing insight into native Everglades culture and language.

Thank you also to my family for their undying patience, laughter, and love. And to my husband, Curtis Sponsler, not only for keeping me fed and alive while I wrote late into the night, but for designing this badass pirate ship cover. Seriously, I couldn't have asked for a more amazing artist and best friend. Lastly, I thank my MacBook Pro for taking a keyboard beating these last 7 years and allowing me to write roughly 40 stories for readers and clients alike. Please don't die on me yet.

Book 1 – Haunted Florida

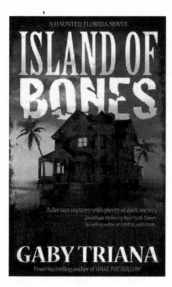

When Ellie Whitaker leaves her dead-end job and ex behind to spread her grandmother's ashes in tropical paradise, the last thing she expected was to face more ghosts of the past.

But darkness lurks inside her grandmother's former home turned resort. Ellie's presence stirs up its energies. As a hurricane creeps closer to the island, she must hurry to discover long-buried truths.

About her treasure-hunting grandfather's death in 1951. About the curse her grandmother left behind. About the innkeeper next door with an evil secret.

And the spectral visions she keeps having. Some there to help her. And some to make sure Ellie becomes a ghostly resident of haunted Key West forever.

Book 3 – Haunted Florida

"Some homes want to be miserable."

A ghostly woman in white. A haunted Victorian home. Witchcraft and Santería from Miami's darker side.

When a mysterious old gentleman enters Kaylin Suarez's trendy new age shop, she hopes he's there to buy incense, some sage, maybe a nice rose quartz pendulum for his wife. Instead, the man pleads for help getting rid of "La Dama de Blanco," a ghostly woman in bloody white dress who has recently begun haunting his 100-year-old Coconut Grove estate.

A newbie witch, Kaylin decides to handle the spirit herself instead of deferring to her paranormal community. When her rituals and spells uncover terrifying secrets hidden in the walls of the estate, Kaylin realizes La Dama de Blanco is only the beginning of the haunted home's evil legacy.

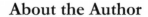

About the Author

GABY TRIANA is the bestselling author of *Island of Bones*, *Cakespell*, *Wake the Hollow*, *Summer of Yesterday*, and many more, as well as 40+ ghostwritten novels for best-selling authors. Gaby has published with HarperCollins, Simon & Schuster, and Entangled, won an IRA Teen Choice Award, ALA Best Paperback Award, and Hispanic Magazine's Good Reads of 2008. She writes about ghosts, haunted places, and abandoned locations. When not obsessing over Halloween, Christmas, or the paranormal, she's taking her family to Disney World, the Grand Canyon, LA, New York, or Key West. Gaby dreams of living in the forests of New England one day but for the meantime resides in sunny Miami with her boys, Michael, Noah, and Murphy, her husband Curtis, their dog, Chloe, and four cats—Daisy, Mickey Meows, Paris, and the reformed thug/shooting survivor, Bowie.

Visit Gaby at **www.GabyTriana.com** and subscribe to her **newsletter**. Also, check out her blog at: **www.WitchHaunt.com.**

Also by Gaby Triana

Horror:

ISLAND OF BONES

RIVER OF GHOSTS

CITY OF SPELLS

Paranormal Young Adult:

WAKE THE HOLLOW

Contemporary Young Adult:

CAKESPELL

SUMMER OF YESTERDAY

RIDING THE UNIVERSE

THE TEMPTRESS FOUR

CUBANITA

BACKSTAGE PASS

Made in the USA
Middletown, DE
02 July 2021